"Lie dow

Quent glowered. "What suddenly gave you the idea that you can order *me* around?"

"You always told me to be prepared to take over if my partner was disabled," Lyndsay replied calmly. From now on it was going to be awfully hard for Quent to treat her in that big-brother way of his. He might try, but she'd do her best to see he didn't succeed.

Quent didn't respond. The more he thought about the way Lyndsay had kissed him when she'd heard they were coming to England, the more he wished he hadn't been so obvious in his response to her. But a person could only stand so much!

Lyndsay, too, fell silent. She stood at the window, looking up at the tower. How did the ghost know to appear just then? She had never heard of a ghost that came out in the daytime. Ghosts weren't real. Every sane person knew that!

Dear Reader,

Sometimes, if you're lucky, you meet a man who is so fascinating you just can't get him out of your mind. That's what happened to me and Luke Thorndike, the lovable, imaginative hero of *Loving Deceiver,* Harlequin Romance #3014. A famous screenwriter, he invents a fictitious assassination plot to keep the woman he loves, Detective Theresa Long, glued to his side. By the time she discovers the ruse, she is Luke's forever.

But I didn't want to let Luke go, for I was hopelessly in love with the rascal, too. What to do? There could never be another Luke. He was totally unique. The answer? Have Luke help another couple with one of his clever schemes.

Theresa's brother, Quent, also a detective, has been courting her best friend, Lyndsay Stuart, but so slowly that Lyndsay is afraid he'll never get to the point of passion. Why is he such a *Reluctant Lover?* Nuptial phobia, says Luke, brought on by investigating so many cases of infidelity. He needs some help. Luke hatches another of his inspired plans and in a matter of days Lyndsay and Quent are in each other's arms. Is the irrepressible Luke through plotting now? I doubt it. I'm still in love with him.

Sincerely,

Katherine Arthur

RELUCTANT LOVER
Katherine Arthur

Harlequin Books

TORONTO • NEW YORK • LONDON
AMSTERDAM • PARIS • SYDNEY • HAMBURG
STOCKHOLM • ATHENS • TOKYO • MILAN
MADRID • WARSAW • BUDAPEST • AUCKLAND

ISBN 0-373-03282-X

Harlequin Romance first edition September 1993

RELUCTANT LOVER

PROLOGUE

"TERRY LOVE!"

"I'm coming!" Theresa Long Thorndike answered the bellow from her husband, Luke. She gathered up the pages of the letter she'd been reading and hurried across the pool deck to the cabana-like building that was the famous screenwriter's office and study. "What's the emergency?" she asked as she entered.

"I needed to see your beautiful face," Luke replied, laughing as Theresa made a grotesque face at him. "Sorry to yell, but I just got a call from Sir Alfred Frobisher, that retired British intelligence chap who's due out here next week to consult with me on turning his memoirs into a screenplay. Seems his wife has tired of the book tour they've been on and wants to go home and tend her prize roses. She doesn't like the idea of going without him, so Alfred's looking for someone interesting to be a companion for her on the trip and keep her entertained until he gets back. You don't happen to know of someone who'd fill the bill, do you? Marian's a delightful lady, and their home, Gravelpick Manor, is a regular museum. Centuries old."

"I don't know anyone offhand, but I'll ask around," Theresa replied. She frowned. "Isn't Gravelpick Manor the place you visited a couple of years ago that has the resident ghost?"

"Right." Luke nodded. "I didn't see him myself, but quite a few ladies claim they have. Seems he was a dashing young Romeo about five hundred years ago and hasn't changed since."

Theresa shuddered. "That might let out a lot of possible candidates for Mrs. Frobisher's companion."

"Seriously?" Luke's eyebrows arched. "Don't tell me my intrepid little detective, vanquisher of murderous mobsters, is afraid of ghosts."

"Terrified," Theresa admitted. "Mobsters are real. Ghosts are . . . I don't know. They just aren't even supposed to be. If I were to see one, I'd probably faint."

"Maybe you shouldn't mention the ghost, then," Luke said. He gestured to the letter in Theresa's hand. "Who's the lengthy epistle from?"

"Lyndsay Stuart," Theresa replied. "She says it's so hot in Chicago they're thinking of changing the name of the A-1 Detective Agency to the Sizzling Sleuths."

"Miserable climate. They should come to California," Luke said. "How's the romance between Lyndsay and your brother? Any more heat generated there yet?"

Theresa shook her head. "Lyndsay says Quent takes her out to dinner fairly often and they have long, serious discussions, but so far he hasn't even kissed her. And when they're working together, it's all business as usual. He bosses her around just like he used to do with me. She's getting tired of that, and I'm afraid she's getting tired of waiting for him to do something besides talk."

"I'm surprised at old Quent," Luke said, frowning. "At our wedding, his eyes lit up like halogen headlights every time he looked at Lyndsay, and she kept staring at him and walking into people. It's been almost six months since she took your place working for Quent. Maybe the spark's faded for him."

"No, it hasn't," Theresa said. "I was wondering about that, too, so last time I talked to him I suggested he set up a date for Lyndsay with Cal Dockstader when he's in Chicago next month. He nearly bit my head off for suggesting it. When I tried to pin him down about why, though, he wouldn't say anything specific. I'm supposed to understand that, quote, these things take time, unquote."

"Maybe Lyndsay's going to have to make the first move," Luke said thoughtfully. "I'm afraid your parents' breakup, plus all of the infidelity he sees in the detective business, have given Quent a bad case of nuptialphobia. Six months without a kiss isn't healthy. He needs his passions aroused a bit."

"I told her almost the same thing, but she says that's not her style, and besides, she's afraid he might fire her if she got too forward. I told her he wouldn't, but..." Theresa sighed. "I'd like to knock their heads together. They need something to get them out of their rut."

"Mmm, yes," Luke said. He stared into space, then a smile slowly spread across his face and he leaned toward Theresa. "I have an idea. What if Marian Frobisher were to have two companions? Not detectives, of course, something undercover. Alfred has a nephew, Freddie..."

For several minutes, Luke outlined his plan while Theresa listened, thinking as she did that his mind was still as clever and devious as when he'd concocted a phony assassination plot to convince her his life was in danger so that she would confess she loved him.

"Well, Terry my sweet, what do you think?" Luke asked when he'd finished. "Shall I see if the Frobishers will go along with it?"

"It might work," Theresa said slowly. "But if Lyndsay and Quent figure out we're behind it, they'll be furious, especially Quent. He'd take it even worse than I did when I found out what you'd done."

Luke chuckled. "Yes, but that was only temporary. Think of the end result. Here we are, basking in wedded bliss, while your poor brother is still having 'long, serious discussions' with the woman he adores. That could go on for years."

"True." Theresa chewed her lip pensively, then suddenly she smiled. "I don't like to meddle, but on the other hand, why not? At worst they'll get a paid vacation in a marvelous place and want to kill both of us. Go ahead, call Sir Alfred."

CHAPTER ONE

"WAKE UP, LYNDSAY."

Lyndsay Stuart's eyes flew open. She turned to look at Quentin Long, whose face was only inches from hers. In the semidarkness, his eyes appeared unnaturally bright, flashing out an aura of tension that seemed to envelop them. For a moment, as she stared into his eyes, she couldn't decide whether she was awake or still caught in a dream of the two of them lying naked on a tropical shore, Quent's green eyes glowing with passion and his sensuous mouth smiling as his face came closer and closer. Then his lips touched hers, sending sparks dancing....

"Are you all right?" he whispered, scanning her face intently. "Will you be able to drive?"

With a sudden jolt, Lyndsay remembered exactly where they were and what they were doing. They were sitting in the front seat of a car, taking turns watching a house that a man, one Barney Kreskil, had entered about an hour ago, at 2:00 a.m. "Oh, yes, I'm fine. Wh-what's happening?" she asked, trying to hide her confusion and disappointment.

"Mrs. Foley's leaving with him," Quent replied, squinting briefly toward the house of the Reverend William Foley, whose suspicions about his wife's activities while he was out of town on business were responsible for their surveillance. He looked back at Lyndsay. "The man's carrying a suitcase. He didn't have one when he went in, did he?''

''No. I would've said so if he did. Do you suppose she's taking off with the guy?''

''Could be. She's in the car. Now he's in. Here they come.'' Quent sank down low, out of sight, and looked toward Lyndsay again. ''Buckle up now. Start the car.''

''Yes, sir,'' Lyndsay said, trying not to sound irritated. After six months, she wished that Quent would at least give her credit for knowing those basic skills. She started the car and then shot up to sitting position. Moments later, she made a U-turn, bumping into the opposite curb slightly as she did.

''Careful,'' Quent said sharply. ''That's hard on the tires.''

''I know that,'' Lyndsay replied tightly. The street was narrow, but she doubted Quent would accept that excuse. No matter how hard she tried, she didn't seem able to make the nondescript old car they used for surveillance turn on a dime the way Quent could.

''Don't get too close,'' Quent warned as they started to follow their quarry down the quiet old suburban street of brick bungalows and square frame houses.

Lyndsay frowned but said nothing. She wasn't too close. She wasn't planning on getting too close. She was more than a block behind the black car.

''They're still going west,'' Quent muttered. ''If he's going to take the expressway, he'll have to turn south in a block or two to catch an interchange. Yep. There he goes. Speed it up a little.''

Lyndsay gritted her teeth and stepped on the gas. Quent really was overdoing the moment-by-moment instructions. Did he think she'd forgotten everything? ''Do you suppose they're heading for the airport?'' she asked as she careened around a corner.

"Maybe. Maybe only a motel near it. The reverend's not due back for a couple of days. Remember, one of the things that bothered him was his wife's not answering the phone a couple of nights when he called. She claimed it was out of order.'' Quent's voice sounded disgusted.

"Poor Mr. Foley,'' Lyndsay said with a sigh. "He seems like a nice man.''

"When did that ever stop anyone?'' Quent asked rhetorically. They turned again, this time onto a busy street that led toward the Tri-State Tollway. "Take it easy. Let that station wagon get between us.''

"I was going to,'' Lyndsay growled, finally unable to suppress a comment. "I *have* done this before, you know.''

"A good detective never stops learning,'' Quent said equably.

Lyndsay bit her lip and refrained from saying it was time Quent learned she wasn't an imbecile. There was no reason for her to be cross, she told herself. He was only trying to be helpful. After all, she had nowhere near the amount of experience he had. Maybe the heat was getting to her. Or maybe it was having Quent so near and yet so far. She was afraid that nights like this, as they saw yet another marriage apparently headed for the rocks, did nothing to help bring him closer, either.

"If they go into O'Hare,'' Quent went on, "they'll probably park in the long-term lot. We'll have to park in a day lot and watch the shuttles. This time of night—''

"If they're looking for O'Hare, they're going the wrong way,'' Lyndsay interrupted as she turned onto the entrance ramp. "They're taking the Tollway north. We may end up in Wisconsin. Maybe old Barney's got a cabin on a lake. Do you suppose they'd invite us to go fishing with them? Maybe if we promised not to tell—''

"Lyndsay!" Quent said sharply, and Lyndsay grinned at him.

"Just kidding," she said. That time she'd known he would scold her. His commitment to honesty and integrity was so strong that he would tolerate no joking about it when they were on a case. She often thought it was something of a contradiction that Quent so openly admired the deceptive plot with which Luke Thorndike had captured his sister Theresa's heart. Theresa's explanation was that Quent thought anyone who'd go to so much trouble to capture the woman he wanted deserved to win her. Lyndsay thought it might have more to do with Quent's admiration for Luke's brilliant, unconventional inventiveness. At the wedding, she'd overheard Quent say he considered Luke a genius for being able to fool both him and Theresa. "I'd hate to have to outwit him," he'd said.

"Watch that semi!" Quent barked, as one of the huge tractor-trailers thundered by and then cut in front of them, a little too close for comfort.

"I *am* watching!" Lyndsay snapped nervously. Having Quent yell like that didn't help her nerves one bit. She glanced in her sideview mirror. "Oh, great, he's got a buddy coming up to join him. We don't need a whole blasted convoy between us."

"Just be patient. When the second one gets on by, pull out and follow him," Quent said a little more calmly.

Lyndsay executed the recommended maneuver, pulling out behind the second semi, which was now cruising along parallel to the first, with no apparent desire to get ahead of it. A construction project had the center lanes blocked off, effectively trapping them behind the pair.

"Flash your lights. Maybe this jerk will get the message," Quent instructed.

"I just did!"

"You needn't shout," Quent said coolly. "I meant you should do it again."

"Oh," Lyndsay said in a small voice. She followed his instructions, wondering if she was just extrasensitive tonight or if Quent was actually being much more short with her than usual. Ordinarily, he was quite calm and slow to anger. But then, she consoled herself, he wasn't usually so tired and uncomfortable. He'd filled in for a sick employee last night, so this was his second night in a row with almost no sleep, and to top it off, the weather was unbearably hot.

During the tense silence that followed, the semi in front of them finally pulled in front of the first one, and Lyndsay shot ahead of them. The black car was nowhere in sight.

"Darn it," Lyndsay said, frowning. "They must have taken that first exit. Either that or they really sped up. I don't see them. How far do you want to go before we give up?"

"May as well take the next exit and head on home," Quent said, his voice raspy with displeasure. "I doubt they'd risk getting a ticket for speeding." Lyndsay could feel his eyes boring into her as he added, "If we'd stayed in the outside lane until that second semi got past the first one, we could have seen if they'd taken that first exit."

"But you said to pull out and follow him!" Lyndsay said. She was sure she'd done what Quent told her. Why was he so determined to find fault with her tonight?

"I said *when* he got by." Quent's voice was growlier than ever. "Perhaps I didn't make myself clear. Remember that the next time."

Lyndsay clenched her jaw and blinked rapidly, hoping Quent wouldn't notice she was fighting back tears. It made her feel silly and childish, but his anger cut like a knife. She hated to have Quent angry with her. Why had she snapped at him? Even worse, why had she been so stupid? She glanced at him apprehensively, but he appeared to have dozed off. Suddenly she felt achingly tired. It was no use, she thought unhappily. She might as well have stayed in Wisconsin.

Lyndsay had come to Chicago from a small Wisconsin town, hoping to escape the ubiquitous reminders of a broken engagement and the tedium of working as a secretary for an elderly lawyer. At first the large Chicago law firm where she'd found a job had seemed exciting, but after three years she realized it was just another dead-end job. About then she met Theresa Long at an exercise class when they caught each other's eye and laughed as they both got one of the movements completely backward. They began going out for coffee after the class and eventually compared notes, Lyndsay learning of Theresa's earlier disastrous affair with the great Lucas Thorndike, and telling Theresa of her own unfortunate experience. Both agreed men were not to be trusted and they would pursue their own careers without one. As their friendship blossomed, however, Lyndsay began to realize Theresa had never gotten over Luke, while her own former fiancé no longer held any part of her heart. She also realized Theresa's work as a detective was much more interesting than her own, something she might want to try herself. By then, Theresa had begun mentioning her brother, Quent—whom Lyndsay *had* to meet—a problem, since Quent steadfastly refused to let Theresa arrange a date for him. "I'm going to get you two together or die trying," Theresa had said only a week before her

excursion to New Orleans on the same train with Luke
Thorndike brought that pair together again. Lyndsay
privately doubted anyone could be as handsome and
wonderful as Theresa made her brother out to be. Then
she met him at Theresa and Luke's wedding, and it felt
as if bells, whistles and sirens all went off inside her at
once. She had thought perhaps he felt something, too,
when he suggested she apply for Theresa's job, but now
she wondered if perhaps that had all been Theresa's idea. Of course, he had taken her out quite often
and they did get along well, but that didn't add up to
wedding bells for them.

"I wish I was home," Lyndsay muttered to herself,
thinking longingly of cool Wisconsin days and long twi-
light hours on the front veranda of the big white house at
the end of Main Street, drinking her mother's special
lemonade and eating big bowls of popcorn with real
butter.

"What did you say?" Quent asked, startling Lyndsay
out of her musings.

"Nothing. Just, I'm home," Lyndsay replied with a
sigh as they arrived at her apartment building. She
stopped the car and looked over at him. He studied her
thoughtfully, but said nothing for so long that at last she
asked, "Now what?"

"Now," he said, finally pushing himself forward and
preparing to get out of the car. "I am going home and
going to bed. I'll send Mitchell and Riggins out to scout
the motels near that first exit in the morning. You can
sleep late, but be in my office by one."

Lyndsay nodded, her heart plummeting. He was too
tired to bawl her out any more tonight, but he was going
to get her in his office tomorrow and do the job right.
They both got out of the car and she watched Quent walk

around to the driver's side. He looked tired and tense.
She wondered if he was thinking that trying to change
Lyndsay Stuart from a legal secretary into a detective was
turning out to be more bother than it was worth, but his
expression was inscrutable as he said, "Good night,
Lyndsay," in a rather flat voice before his broad shoulders edged through the car door and he lowered himself
into the driver's seat.

"G-good night," Lyndsay said shakily. She turned
quickly away and, head down, hurried toward the security door of her apartment building. Tears welled in her
eyes and began to spill down her cheeks. It was hopeless.
She might as well go back to Wisconsin. Quent's only real
interest was his work. He had taken her off the Foley
case, didn't care if she came in late, probably planned to
fire her, anyway. She bent and fumbled in her purse for
her key, then let out a little scream as a hand came down
on her shoulder.

"Don't panic, it's only me," said a deep voice.

"Quent!" she gasped, whirling around, her heart racing. "I thought you'd gone."

Quent shook his head. "I could see you were unhappy, the way you walked all hunched over." He bent
toward Lyndsay and peered into her face, his forehead
creased in a worried frown. "You're crying," he said, his
own expression becoming even more anxious. "What's
wrong, Lyndsay?"

The gentle, sympathetic look on Quent's face played
havoc with Lyndsay's attempts to stifle her tears. "I'm
s-so stupid that now you're fed up with me and you've
t-taken me off the F-Foley case," she choked out between suppressed sobs.

"Oh, Lyndsay, is that what you thought?" Quent
looked stricken. When Lyndsay nodded dumbly, he

brushed a tear from her cheek with his fingertips. "I'm sorry," he said, his eyes suddenly velvety soft through the blur of her tears. "I was much too harsh with you tonight. Overtired, I guess. I'm not taking you off the Foley case. Something's come up and we have to turn it over to someone else. Okay?" He smiled cajolingly.

"I—I guess so. What's come up?" Lyndsay replied dubiously, her eyes now resting on his lips. The only thing she was sure of was that she wished he would kiss her. If only she had the courage to take Theresa's advice and kiss him first, but she was afraid. . . .

"Maybe I'll tell you the secret I was going to surprise you with tomorrow," Quent said, studying her thoughtfully.

"Secret? What secret?" A whole array of romantic secret pronouncements she would like to have Quent surprise her with raced through her mind.

"We're going to England soon to protect the wife of a wealthy friend of Luke Thorndike's," Quent replied. "A fantastic old manor house somewhere in the north."

"To England? Honestly? Oh, Quent, that's wonderful!" She smiled radiantly as he nodded, all of her worries gone.

Just what it was that triggered her rash decision, Lyndsay wasn't sure. Perhaps it was watching the smile lines crinkle around Quent's tired eyes and his lips curve upward in pleasure, and knowing he was happy to have pleased her. Maybe it was the warmth in his beautiful jade-green eyes that made her feel as if the sun had come out. Whatever it was, suddenly she could stand it no longer. She flung her arms around his neck and kissed him.

The moment her lips touched Quent's, Lyndsay knew from the shimmering waves of excitement that coursed

through her that she had been right about how it would
feel. His mouth was deliciously warm, yielding softly to
the pressure of her kiss. She hadn't planned on more than
a brief touch, hadn't really thought at all past the overwhelming desire to finally end her endless longing. But,
as the shock waves built inside her, she clung to Quent's
neck, unable to make herself break away. The vague
thought that she was probably doing something very
wrong from the viewpoint of her future as a detective
wandered through her mind and then vanished as Quent's
arms closed around her and he responded to her kiss with
an intensity that left her breathless. Behind her closed
eyelids, clouds of sparkling particles seemed to whirl her
into a dizzying vortex of delight. Quent's hand plunged
into her thick, dark curls, holding her head close as he
angled his mouth back and forth, exploring and seeking
as if he would devour her. Lyndsay clung ever more
tightly to him, reveling in the sensation of his hard male
body against her soft curves. When his hand left her head
and slid around between them, then began slowly caressing her through the soft fabric of her shirt, a little moan
of sheer ecstasy escaped from her throat.

As if she had cried out for help, Quent pulled his head
back and stared at her, then jerked his hand away and
stepped back. His expression was so confused that
Lyndsay wondered for a moment if her cry had actually
frightened him. "I'm sorry," he said hoarsely, still staring at her as he shook his head back and forth. "I don't
know what came over me. We...that is, I...shouldn't
have done that. We can't work together and do...that
sort of thing." He raised his chin and essayed a more firm
expression. "I promise, I won't let it happen again. I expect you to promise to, uh, keep your distance, also."

Expect all you want to, Lyndsay thought, her heart still pounding from the intensity of Quent's response. *I plan to do everything in my power to see that it does happen again!* However, now was definitely not the time to let him know that, so Lyndsay crossed her fingers behind her. "Oh, yes, I promise," she said as soberly and as convincingly as she could. "I certainly do."

Quent took a deep breath, then let it out in a rush. "I apologize again," he said, trying for a rueful smile and, Lyndsay thought, not succeeding. "It must be the lack of sleep. I don't usually lose control of myself like that."

"I think the heat got to both of us," Lyndsay said, her voice oozing sympathy. "Maybe you should sleep in in the morning, too."

"I wish I could." Quent sighed. "But I've got to finish making arrangements for our absence. I expect we'll be going quite soon. The Englishman—his name is Sir Alfred Frobisher—is coming in tomorrow at one to fill us in on the problem. Luke only gave me a sketchy report."

"We get to meet him tomorrow? How exciting," Lyndsay said. "Sir Alfred. He's been knighted?"

"Yes. Service to the Crown back in World War II, I believe," Quent replied. "Well, I'd better be going. I meant it—you don't need to come in until one if you don't want to. You need your rest. Remember to take your vitamins, too, so you won't be a sitting duck for the summer flu. You wouldn't want to spoil our trip."

"No, I certainly wouldn't." When Quent made no move to leave, instead standing still and looking at her as if he were hypnotized, she finally added, "Good night, then. Sleep well. But not until you get home."

Quent came out of his trance at that. "Uh, yes. I'm sure I will," he said. "I'll see you tomorrow."

With that, he turned, crossed to his car and got in. Lyndsay watched, smiling as he drove away. When he was out of sight, she turned to the door, unlocked it, then hurried up the stairs to her apartment. When she'd bolted the door behind her, she let out a whoop of joy and spun around until she was so dizzy that she tumbled onto the sofa.

QUENT DROVE HOME slowly, his exhausted body aching as if it had been battered by a tidal wave. *I can't let myself lose control like that,* he thought one minute, then the next he was reliving that kiss and wishing he was holding Lyndsay in his arms again. His mind continued in that orbit until he'd parked and climbed the stairs with painful slowness to his own apartment.

A cold shower temporarily soothed him. He'd be fine tomorrow, back in control, he told himself as he lay on his bed, staring at the ceiling. He would go back to his plan, which he'd worked out almost the moment he met her. First, spend as much time as possible with Lyndsay so he'd be absolutely sure how deep his feelings for her ran before he indulged in more physical contact. Then, when he was sure, some serious, passionate courting. She was so desirable it would be far too easy to get carried away. Those big, dark eyes of hers. The adorable way her soft, rosy lips curved, and they had tasted even more delicious...

Quent passed a shaking hand over his tired eyes. "Don't think about that," he muttered. "Stay cool. Take your time. Nothing really happened. It was just a kiss." But good Lord, how it had made him feel! She'd felt it, too, he knew she had. But could she love him? Or was it only physical attraction? He knew she was attracted to him from the way he sometimes caught her watching him, but she was usually the epitome of professional restraint when they were together. Why had she kissed him so suddenly? Of course, she was excited about the prospect of going to England. He was excited himself, and not only because he hadn't been there before. Part of it, he admitted with a wry smile, was the idea of having Lyndsay with him, all to himself, watching her bright-eyed enthusiasm about seeing new things. How lucky that Luke Thorndike...

The smile changed slowly to a frown. Was it luck? Theresa had been asking how he and Lyndsay were getting along. She had wanted to get him together with Lyndsay for a long time, even before they'd finally met at the wedding. Luke was a clever, romantic devil. Could this be another of his bizarre matchmaking plots? Could Lyndsay be in on it, too? She might have been getting frustrated with the slow pace of his courtship. She and Theresa still kept in close touch....

Quent sat up in bed, his eyes narrowed in anger. If that was what was going on, he was damned if he'd go along with it! But how could he find out? Luke and Theresa would never tell, and if he accused Lyndsay and it wasn't, he'd look like a fool! He got up and stomped into his kitchen for a glass of ice water, then sat down at the table, staring blankly out the window, his mind a churning mass of conflicting thoughts: Alfred was no actor. Why would he pay them to protect Marian if she didn't need it? Luke could be trying out a new story idea—he'd turned his and Theresa's story into a screenplay. Was he just being paranoid? Luke and Theresa and Lyndsay wouldn't—or would they? Quent was still sitting there when the sun came up.

CHAPTER TWO

LYNDSAY LAY on the sofa, smiling to herself as the room continued to spin around her. Quent had kissed her, and no matter what he'd said about being overtired, she was sure he'd felt something powerful. From now on it was going to be awfully hard for him to treat her in that big-brother way of his. He might try, but she was going to do her best to see he didn't succeed. What would be the best way to do that?

Lyndsay got up from the sofa and walked slowly into her bedroom, unbuttoning her still-damp shirt as she went. She pulled it off and flung it onto her bed, then looked at herself in the mirror. She had a nicely rounded figure, which was disguised by the plain tailored shirts and slacks she usually wore. With no makeup and her dark hair pulled back and anchored with a clip at the back of her head, she looked barely twenty-one, let alone twenty-seven. When she'd gone out to dinner with Quent, she'd dressed conservatively and worn little makeup, afraid he might question her motives in applying for Theresa's old job if she turned into an after-hours siren.

That situation, Lyndsay decided, had gone on long enough. The fact that she had fallen for him like the proverbial ton of bricks the moment she'd laid eyes on him at Theresa's wedding and practically turned cartwheels when he suggested she might like to apply to replace his sister was beside the point. Quent should know by now she had sincerely hated her old job and intended to become a thoroughly competent detective, but after that kiss there was no way she could disguise the fact that she was interested in him as a man, too. Of course, he was perfectly right to say they couldn't let any emotional involvement interfere with their work, but when they weren't working... Lyndsay frowned thoughtfully. Quent required her to wear sturdy, simple clothes at work, but tomorrow was going to be different. Meeting Sir Alfred Frobisher was an occasion that called for something special. Maybe her dark red silk? She went to her closet and pulled the dress out. Perfect, she thought, smiling to herself. It was cool and sleeveless and fairly low-cut, very plain but nicely fitted. Quent shouldn't find fault with it for the occasion, and it ought to make him remember that kiss.

Humming softly to herself, Lyndsay took a shower and got ready for bed. She wasn't desperately tired now, but she was glad that Quent had said she didn't have to come in till one. That would give her plenty of time to get ready and look her best. She set her alarm for ten, then got into bed and stretched contentedly. So far, this day was turning out far better than she'd ever dreamed it would. If only it could keep going as well!

When she awoke, Lyndsay did her hair with special care, leaving it hanging loose in deep, soft curls. She added a touch of blusher and some eye shadow and mascara. Satisfied she no longer looked like someone who needed to be reminded to take their vitamins, she called a taxi to take her to the downtown Loop. This was not a day to get rumpled and hot on the bus.

It was a quarter to one when Lyndsay sailed in the door of the A-1 Detective Agency. "Hi, Angie, how's it going?'' she said to the beautiful blond receptionist who had become a good friend.

"Wow!" Angie said, her big blue eyes flying wide open. "You look terrific. I like that outfit. With your dark hair and those big gold hoops in your ears, you look like a gypsy. Something special going on?"

"Thanks, and yes," Lyndsay replied. "We're meeting a special English client today. Is the boss in?"

Angie shook her head. "No, he's still on his lunch break." She leaned toward Lyndsay and beckoned with her finger.

"What?" Lyndsay asked, coming closer.

"Did something happen last night? I mean, something between you and the boss?" Angie asked in confidential tones.

Startled by Angie's perceptiveness, Lyndsay fought back a blush. "No, of course not," she replied, trying to look offended. "Why?"

"Well, Mr. Long called me this morning at about seven and asked if I could come in early, by eight o'clock. I did, and he was already here. He looked like death warmed over, and he was cross as a bear." Angie twisted her carefully sculptured lips in a wry grimace. "He nearly bit my head off when I couldn't find the Warburton file right away. I've never seen him so uptight. Something's really gotten under his skin."

"Oh, dear," Lyndsay said, frowning. "Maybe it's because I lost the trail of our suspect. He was pretty angry about that." But Quent hadn't seemed angry when he'd left her. A little unnerved by their kiss, maybe, but not angry. What could have happened in the meantime? From Angie's description, it didn't sound as if he'd gotten any sleep at all.

"Could be, but I doubt it," Angie replied. "I think it's more serious than that." She eyed Lyndsay speculatively. "I thought maybe spending the night alone with one of the prettiest girls in Chicago had finally worn through that big-brother attitude of his. If I know anything about men, it's going to hit him like a ton of bricks when it happens. You're sure nothing happened?"

Lyndsay shook her head, amazed at Angie's astute analysis but not quite ready to confess anything that intimate to her, even though she had told Angie in the past that being treated like a little sister was wearing pretty thin. "I think he's just tired and has a lot to do to get ready for our trip to England," she said. "He had stakeouts two nights in a row."

"I know he's tired," Angie said dryly, "but you'd think he was planning to go to the jungles of Africa or something the way he's fussing over every little detail of who's going to do what while he's gone. It's not as if they don't have telephones in England." She glanced toward the glass outer door. "Uh-oh. Here he comes."

As Quent burst through the door, Lyndsay noted he was wearing one of his nicest summer suits, a light gray with a pinstripe, and a deep red tie almost the same color as her dress. The look he wore, however, was not one of his best. He seemed terribly tired, and his mouth was drawn tight, his usual expression when he was angry or disgusted. His eyes, when they fell on Lyndsay, were glacial green pools.

"Are you just stopping by on your way to a party?" he asked sarcastically, looking her up and down.

Stung, Lyndsay raised her chin defiantly and glared back at him. "No," she replied. "I'm dressed to meet Sir Alfred, and I'm also trying to stay cool on a day when it's supposed to be over a hundred degrees outside. In case you hadn't noticed, the air-conditioning in this old building can't quite keep up in this kind of weather.''

Quent made a noncommittal sort of grunting noise and turned toward his office. "You may as well come in," he said over his shoulder. "Sir Alfred should be here anytime now."

"All right," Lyndsay said. She glanced apprehensively at Angie, who gave her a knowing smile. Good Lord, she thought as she followed Quent into his office, could Angie be right? If so, she wasn't sure that kiss was worth it, after all. Big-brother Quent was better than this glacial beast.

No sooner had Quent closed the door behind them than he looked down disapprovingly at Lyndsay's white sandals. "Why on earth are you wearing such flimsy shoes?" he asked. "I thought I had made it clear that they're not appropriate here. You couldn't possibly pursue a suspect in those things."

Even Angie's description of Quent's ill temper had not prepared Lyndsay for such a continued personal attack, especially when she'd done nothing to deserve it. Her shoes were perfectly suitable for today's occasion. "I don't expect to have to pursue Sir Alfred," she said coldly. "You're dressed up to meet him. Why shouldn't I be?"

"Because you look—" Quent began, then stopped abruptly, turned and went to his desk. "Sit down and let's go over what you'll need to take to England," he said, shuffling through a pile of papers in front of him before he glanced up at Lyndsay and asked, "Do you have a valid passport?"

Still wondering what Quent had been about to say about how she looked, Lyndsay answered, "Yes, I have a passport. You asked me that when I came to work for you, remember? You said I should have one just in case, so I got one.''

''Good,'' Quent said, glancing at her briefly again. ''Now, it's apt to be quite a bit cooler there. You'll need sweaters and slacks, but try not to overdo it. Just a few changes of underwear and maybe one dressy outfit. There's no point in dragging along a huge suitcase full of things you'll never need. But don't forget your multiple vitamins. They've been shown to be a useful antidote to the effects of jet lag.''

For a moment Lyndsay could think of nothing to say except some sarcastic remark that would probably get her in deep trouble with Quent. Did he actually think he needed to tell her exactly what to pack? At last she said stiffly, ''I am quite capable of doing my own packing.''

''Every woman on earth needs reminding not to over-pack,'' Quent replied. ''Besides, you haven't traveled much.''

Lyndsay was about to say she didn't realize Quent was that intimate with all the world's women when a sudden thought struck her. If Angie was right, maybe Quent had been so unnerved by that kiss that now he was trying to reassert his big-brother relationship with her! He certainly looked as if something had kept him awake all night. Would he admit it if it had? She gave him a sympathetic smile. ''I do appreciate your advice,'' she said, ''but try not to worry. You look as if you didn't sleep at all last night. Was something bothering you?''

Quent's head jerked up and he stared at her. ''Of course not. I slept just fine,'' he said. ''Not enough, but I'm all right. I don't need fussing over.''

So much for that, Lyndsay thought wryly. He wouldn't admit he hadn't slept, and when she showed any concern for him, she was ''fussing.'' ''I'm glad to hear it,'' she said. "Then I won't ask you if you've been taking your vitamins so you won't get physically run down."

Quent scowled, and just as he opened his mouth as if he was about to make a sharp retort, his intercom warbled. He answered Angie with a curt, "Yes?"

"Sir Alfred Frobisher is here," she said.

"Send him right in," Quent said. Still frowning, he got up and went to shake hands with the man who entered as Angie opened his door.

Sir Alfred Frobisher, Lyndsay thought, as she, too, stood up to greet him, looked exactly as she would have imagined a character from Dickens in modern dress. He was short and rotund, his cheeks round and rosy, his head bald except for a fringe of white hair.

"I'm very pleased to meet you, Sir Alfred," Quent said, managing, to Lyndsay's relief, to abandon his frown for a warm smile. He gestured toward Lyndsay. "This is my associate, Lyndsay Stuart."

"Just call me Alfred," he said. "The 'sir' tends to make people a bit standoffish." He moved toward Lyndsay with his hand outstretched. "A great pleasure, Ms. Stuart. Luke told me you were stunning. And I thought it was only on the telly that detectives had such glamorous assistants."

"You're too kind," Lyndsay murmured as he gripped her hand firmly. "Quent told me you're a friend of Luke Thorndike's, but he didn't say how you happened to be acquainted with him."

"I was a consultant on that spy thriller he wrote several years ago," Alfred replied. "I was in British intelligence in World War II, you see. Luke came to England to stay with me for a while, and later he encouraged me to write my memoirs, which is the reason I'm here today."

"Why don't you have a seat and tell us exactly what it is we can do for you?" Quent said. "All Luke told me was that it involves protecting your wife."

"That's right," Alfred said, smiling as he lowered his girth into a seat. "Let's get right down to business. Best way to do things, I always say. As I was saying, I wrote my memoirs. A publisher snapped them up and they've had me on a publicity tour in this country for several weeks. There's a lot of exciting material in my book, so Luke's going to turn it into a screenplay. Of course, I want to see it's done right, so after I finish my publicity stint here in Chicago, I'm going to California for a short time to get Luke off on the right foot. And that, my friends, brings me to the problem our mutual friend Luke suggested you two could solve. You see, my wife, Marian, has been accompanying me on the tour, but she's eager to go home to Gravelpick Manor now and tend her prize roses instead of going on to California. I don't want her going alone. I'm afraid my nephew, Freddie, is not to be trusted. He tried to borrow some money from Marian before we left, and I absolutely put my foot down—Freddie's a spendthrift and a gambler, hangs around with all kinds of lowlifes—and he was extremely upset. He acted as if his very life depended upon his getting the money, which, if he's run up some nasty gambling debts, it well might."

When Alfred finally paused for breath and raised his bushy eyebrows meaningfully, Lyndsay asked, "Are you worried he might try again to persuade her when you're not there?"

"Worse than that, I'm afraid," Alfred said, shaking his head, his eyes squinted grimly. "Much worse."

"Oh, my," Lyndsay said, horrified. "Do you mean physical violence?"

Alfred nodded. "I do indeed. You see, Marian's a wealthy woman in her own right. A former stage star. Lovely woman. A bit younger than I. I couldn't live without her. But she's never been able to see that Freddie's no good. His parents passed on when he was a young teenager, and since he's my brother's son, I took him in. He and I never hit it off, but Marian's been like a mother to him, let him take advantage of her good nature right and left. He persuaded her to put half her estate in his name. Told her I'd probably let him starve if anything happened to her, which isn't far from the mark. I'd have sent him packing years ago, but she wouldn't hear of it, so he hangs around Gravelpick Manor whenever he gets bored with playing storekeeper in London or runs out of money, both of which happen frequently."

"What do you mean, playing storekeeper?" Quent asked.

"He runs a little specialty shop where he puts together elaborate stereo systems and the like for people who can afford the best," Alfred replied. "He's a whiz at electronics. If he weren't so blasted lazy, he could make his own fortune at it. As it is, he'd rather play at it when it suits him and wait to inherit his share of Marian's estate. Or not wait, as the case may be. I don't think he's the type to go in for mayhem ordinarily, but if his own miserable skin is on the line . . . well, I'd rather not take the chance. As I said before, Marian means everything to me. What I'd like you to do is to travel back to the U.K. with Marian and watch over her until I get back. I'll pay you well, and it should only be a matter of two weeks at the most."

"That sounds like a perfectly reasonable request," Quent said. "We'd be happy to accommodate you."

"Well, there is one other little thing," Alfred said, looking rather uncomfortable. "You see, it wouldn't do for Marian to know you two were detectives. If she thought I'd hired you to protect her from her precious Freddie, she'd have a fit. So Luke suggested you could pretend to be archaeologists, doing some research in the region around Gravelpick Manor. It's an excellent location for that kind of thing. Near North Twickham. We've even got an eleventh-century ruin on the property. If you'd go along with the scheme, I'd introduce you to Marian as a pair of archaeologists I met at the Natural History Museum, which is where she thinks I am today, who just happen to be about to travel to the U.K. for some research and whom I invited to stay at the manor. Marian would be delighted to have company while I'm gone. She loves to entertain. Probably throw a party or two in your honor. I hope that, uh, little condition doesn't make it too difficult for you?" He looked hopefully first at Quent and then at Lyndsay.

Quent eyed Lyndsay and rubbed his chin thoughtfully. "Well, I don't know much about archeology, but I expect we could study enough to be convincing if we have time. It should be an interesting experience, to say the least. When would you want us to go, Mr. Frobisher?"

"I'm scheduled to leave for California the day after tomorrow," Alfred replied. "I know that's terribly short notice, but Marian would like to go home as soon as possible, and I'd rather she didn't have to stay alone in the hotel."

"I think we can manage," Lyndsay put in quickly as Quent frowned doubtfully. "I went on an archaeological dig at an Indian site once, and I can find some books and make us some quick crib notes."

"In that case, I think we can do it," Quent agreed.

"Excellent," Alfred said, beaming happily. "Do you suppose you two could join Marian and me for dinner tonight? I know she'll be eager to meet you once I've broken the good news to her."

"We'd be happy to," Quent said. "We're looking forward to meeting your wife. Now, about the plane reservations..."

While Quent and Alfred Frobisher went into the details of their travel plans, Lyndsay sat quietly and watched Quent. He seemed in perfectly good humor now. Of course, he wouldn't be short-tempered with a client unless he was really deranged, but it was a relief to know he wasn't so upset that he couldn't pull himself together when the occasion demanded. She would hate to think that one kiss could completely unsettle him.

A few minutes later, after Quent showed Alfred to the door and returned to his desk, she was not so sure. His expression was grim as he said, "Well, so you're already an expert on archeology. Good for you. I'm not. I want you to go to the library and make me some cram notes and meet me back here about five. We may have to be able to fool Marian Frobisher this evening, you know. Meanwhile I have to go to my bank and take care of some business. I hadn't planned on having to leave so quickly."

"I think I'll try to find some maps to copy," Lyndsay said. "That should help us zero in on the area near North Twickham."

"Yes, do that," Quent said. He got up from his chair and stumbled as he rounded the corner of his desk. "Damn," he said, rubbing his forehead with one hand and clutching the desk with the other.

"What's wrong, Quent?" Lyndsay asked anxiously. "Are you dizzy?" His face was pale and the dark smudges under his eyes had taken on a bluish cast. When he didn't answer, but continued to hang on to the desk, she took hold of his arm. "Let me help you over to your lounge chair."

"No, no, I'm all right," he said, pulling away from her hand. "I just stood up too quickly." he took a step forward, then stopped again and reached for Lyndsay's arm. "Good Lord," he said, licking his lips nervously. "I can't seem to shake it off. I'm seeing little bright flashes all around."

"You're exhausted, that's what's the matter," Lyndsay said. "I've had that happen to me before. Come on, lean on me and we'll walk slowly over to your sofa. You need a rest."

"I can't. I don't have time—" Quent began, but Lyndsay interrupted.

"You will," she said firmly, "or I'll call the rescue squad and we'll have you in the hospital in nothing flat. I mean it, Quent," she added as he glared at her. "Come on, put your arm across my shoulders." She slid beneath his arm and he reluctantly leaned on her.

"I feel like a fool, leaning on a woman tottering alone in those ridiculous shoes," he grumbled as they moved toward the corner of his office, which was decorated as a small sitting area, with a sofa, lounge chair and coffee table.

"I'd look a lot more ridiculous wearing tennis shoes with this dress, which, I might point out, is exactly the right thing to wear for dinner with the Frobishers," Lyndsay replied. As Quent sat down heavily on the sofa, she piled the throw pillows at one end and went on, "Now, take off your jacket and tie and shoes and lie down. A couple of hours' sleep and you'll feel a lot better."

"Stop clucking at me like a mother hen," Quent snapped as he took off his jacket and handed it to Lyndsay. "I'll take a short rest, that's all. I have to get to the bank." He removed his tie and put it into her outstretched hand. "Hang those up carefully. I don't want them wrinkled."

"Yes, sir," Lyndsay said. She took them to the antique brass coat tree in the corner behind his desk and put them carefully on a hanger. When she turned around, Quent was lying on his back with his shoes still on, staring at the ceiling. His arms were folded stiffly across his chest and his eyebrows were drawn together in a frown. He looked, Lyndsay thought as she drew nearer, as if every muscle in his body was as tense as a coiled spring.

"I can't take time out," he said suddenly, swinging his feet to the floor and sitting up. "There's too much to do. I feel all right now." He jumped to his feet, then, as Lyndsay watched, let out a sort of strangled gasp and swayed toward the coffee table.

Heavens, Lyndsay thought, *he's going to fall and kill himself on one of those sharp corners!* In two quick strides she reached him and used her momentum to push him onto the sofa again. He landed with a crash, with Lyndsay on top of him, in a tangle of arms and legs. "Sorry," she said, looking down into his face and struggling to free herself. "I didn't want you to hit your head on the coffee table. You really must lie down for a while."

Quent's office door opened. "What happened?" came Angie's voice. "Oh, sorry!" The door closed again.

Lyndsay glanced toward the door. Oh, great, she thought. She looked back at Quent, whose face had regained its normal color and then some. His expression was somewhere between embarrassed and furious, but for some reason Lyndsay couldn't fathom, the situation suddenly struck her as hilarious. She started to laugh.

"It isn't funny," Quent snapped, pushing her away. "I don't know what's gotten into you lately, but I won't have you undermining the discipline of this agency."

"I'm sorry," Lyndsay gasped, standing up and grinning down at him. "Don't worry. I'll tell Angie what happened. Now, are you going to lie down and stay put, or do I have to get her in here to help me hold you down?"

"Just go away," Quent growled.

"Lie down first," Lyndsay said firmly.

"No!"

Lyndsay smiled slyly. "Do it, or I'll scream and then tell lies about what was going on."

Quent glowered. "What in hell suddenly gave you the idea you can order me around?" he asked as he stretched out on his side.

"You always told me to be prepared to take over if my partner was disabled," Lyndsay replied calmly as she took the crocheted throw that lay folded on the back of the sofa and shook it open, "and you are definitely disabled. There." She tucked the throw around his shoulders and bent close to his ear. "Now close your eyes and go to sleep," she said softly, "and I'll wake you in time to go over some notes before dinner."

Quent cast Lyndsay a defiant look, but said nothing. He still seemed tense, apparently resigned to her ministrations but a long way from appreciating them. Well, she could put up with that for the time being, as long as he did get some rest. If he didn't, he might get really sick and they wouldn't get to go to England, after all. After she'd heard Sir Alfred's story, that was a trip Lyndsay would almost rather die than miss.

"Close your eyes," she repeated, and this time Quent actually obeyed with no further complaints. He looked so appealing, with his thick, dusky lashes fanned out against his cheeks and a lock of hair falling across his forehead, that Lyndsay was terribly tempted to bend over and kiss him, but she managed to restrain herself by turning and walking quickly to the door. There was no point in pushing her luck, at least not until they were safely at Gravelpick Manor, or unless Quent gave some further sign that his kiss had meant what it felt as if it had. From the way he had been acting today, that didn't seem likely.

QUENT OPENED one eye and watched her go. Was she or wasn't she involved in some kind of plot with Luke and his sister to bring the two of them together? Alfred's story sounded plausible enough, but Luke was very clever, and the more Quent had thought about the way Lyndsay had suddenly kissed him last night when she heard they were going to England, the more suspicious he'd become. That was a lot more than a happy, surprised kiss. It was passionate, almost triumphant, as if it were something she had been planning for a long time. He wished he hadn't been so obvious in his response to her, but damn it all, a man could stand just so much frustration. He wanted her desperately, but he also wanted to do things his own way and not be pushed into anything hurried. When he married, he wanted to be sure it would last.

He pushed the pillows into a more comfortable shape, sighed heavily and closed his eyes. Lyndsay's face, framed by soft curls of shining dark hair, swam mistily before his closed eyelids. How beautiful she looked today. If he didn't get some rest he might really lose control and do something he'd regret. A half hour snooze ought to do it....

CHAPTER THREE

"FOR GOODNESS' SAKE, what happened?" Angie asked as Lyndsay came through Quent's door, then closed it quietly behind her and stood still, leaning limply against the frame. "It looked pretty interesting."

"Shh," Lyndsay said, shaking her head and putting her finger to her lips. She tiptoed to Angie's desk. "Quent's hardly had any sleep in the past two and a half days, and he got so dizzy when he stood up suddenly that he almost fell over. I caught him and then fell over on the sofa with him. He said he had too much to do to take a nap, but I think I finally persuaded him. See that he isn't disturbed, will you?"

"Sure thing," Angie said. She made a wry face. "Too bad it wasn't what it looked like. But I still think it's more than duty calling that has our esteemed boss so wound up. I'll bet he'll be losing a lot more sleep in the near future."

"I'm not so sure of that," Lyndsay replied. "Before Sir Alfred arrived, the only thing on his mind was the trip—he spent the whole time telling me exactly what I should pack. Well, I've got to get moving and do some quick research. We have to be able to sound like archaeologists by tonight. It turns out the job in England is sort of undercover."

"Wow," Angie said, "undercover, too! How neat! What's the boss think of that angle?"

"Not much, I'm afraid," Lyndsay replied with a grimace. "He's added learning about archaeology to the things that have him worried about the trip. I'd better make some really good notes, or he'll bite my head off. I sure hope he gets a decent nap and wakes up with a better attitude."

"He probably will," Angie said comfortingly. "Oh, by the way, Luke Thorndike called and wants Mr. Long to call him back. If he doesn't wake up before I leave, be sure he does that."

"I will," Lyndsay said with a nod. "See you later." She hurried out of the office, frowning to herself. Why would Luke Thorndike want to talk to Quent? Was he afraid he wouldn't take the case when he found out about the archaeology thing?

Lyndsay smiled wryly to herself and pushed the elevator button. She didn't really know much about archaeology, either, but she was glad she'd mentioned her one little experience with it. She'd have said she knew something about nuclear physics if that was what it would have taken to be sure she got to go to England and have Quent to herself for a couple of weeks!

She had scarcely gone a block from the office building when a display in a bookstore window caught her eye: Digging up the Past was the sign on a backdrop that featured a picture of a surprised-looking dinosaur peering over an ancient castle wall. It would be far better, she decided, to have some books they could take with them, instead of only some sketchy notes. A half hour later she was on her way back to the agency with a bag full of books and some maps to help pinpoint the sites they would need to know about.

"Are you going to be able to get that report on the Dunston Manufacturing Company investigation finished before you go?'' Angie asked as she hurried past her.

Lyndsay stopped. ''Eek, I'd forgotten about that. I'll take it home and work on it tonight and have it for you in the morning. Any sign of Quent?''

Angie shook her head. ''Not a peep. He must be sound asleep. I hope he appreciates your concern and isn't crabbier than ever because you've kept him from his chores.''

''I hope so, too,'' Lyndsay said with a sigh, ''but if he doesn't get at least a couple of hours' sleep he may collapse. He seems worried about getting to the bank, but he can do that in the morning. I plan to wake him at five. If he yells at me it's just too bad.''

''You're braver than I am,'' Angie said. ''Just let me get out of here before you prod the beast. I'll leave him a list of the calls he needs to make.''

''He can call Luke Thorndike after five,'' Lyndsay said. ''It's two hours earlier in California.''

She went into her office, took out her new books and tried to banish the thoughts of how Quent might react to sleeping away the afternoon. At the moment, she had a more pressing problem, that of turning the two of them into instant archaeologists. If she couldn't pull that off, Quent might decide to back out of the assignment. It was almost five o'clock, and she had just had Angie type a set of short, informative paragraphs into her computer, then print them out when Angie's intercom warbled.

''Uh-oh,'' Angie said, giving Lyndsay a grim look. She pressed the button. ''Yes, Mr. Long?'' she said softly.

''What in the devil have you been doing all afternoon?'' roared Quent's voice. ''Haven't I had any calls?''

"A few. Nothing important," Angie replied. "Ms. Stuart told me not to disturb you," she added as Lyndsay pointed at herself.

"Since when do you take orders from Ms. Stuart?" came another roar.

Lyndsay shook her head at Angie and held her finger to her lips. "Stop yelling at Angie," she said. "You needed a nap. Why don't you come into my office and see what I've got on archaeology? I'd bring it into your office, but I've got some maps spread out for you to look at."

There was a moment of silence, followed by a growled, "In a few minutes. Angie, bring me the list of who called."

"Yes, sir," Angie said, heaving an audible sigh of relief as she picked up the list and hurried toward Quent's office.

Lyndsay returned to her own little cubicle. At least she had gotten Angie off of the hook, but it remained to be seen what Quent would say to her when he had her alone.

It was half an hour before Quent appeared at her door, plenty of time for Lyndsay to speculate further on how angry he might be with her and also to realize there was now less than an hour for him to pick up enough information to sound as if he knew something about the archaeological sites of northern England. She turned, biting her lip apprehensively at the sound of his footsteps and was relieved to see he looked more thoughtful than angry.

"What's up?" she asked as he came into her office and sat down in the chair next to her desk. He was in his shirtsleeves, his collar unbuttoned and his hair less neatly combed than usual. He didn't seem as tired, Lyndsay thought, but he looked so adorably tousled and still somewhat sleepy that she had to take a deep breath to try to keep her mind from wandering into forbidden territory.

"I just had a talk with Luke Thorndike," he replied, running his fingers around the inside of his collar in a nervous gesture. "He said not to be surprised if Gravelpick Manor isn't quite what one would expect an English country house to be like. I told him I didn't have any expectations about it and asked him to elaborate, but he wouldn't, except to say that the Frobishers are a bit eccentric. Did you get the impression Alfred was eccentric?"

Lyndsay shrugged. "Not really. Maybe a little paranoid about his nephew, Freddie. Did Luke say anything about him?"

Quent shook his head. "I asked him if he'd met him. He said not in the flesh and then laughed, whatever that means. Luke seems to delight in being cryptic."

"Maybe Freddie's a ghost," Lyndsay suggested. "Lots of those old English houses have them. Maybe Alfred just imagines he's after his wife's money."

Quent's frown darkened. "Don't be ridiculous. Ghosts don't exist. Alfred would have to be a lot worse than eccentric to believe anything like that. Still, I did have the feeling that Luke was hiding something. I hope he's not up to some kind of mischief again. Do you think he might be?"

"What kind of mischief?" Lyndsay asked.

"We-e-ell . . ." Quent made a sort of grimace and then shrugged. "Nothing."

"If you mean you think Luke might have persuaded Sir Alfred to go to the expense of having his wife protected from a ghost, of course not," Lyndsay said quickly, seeing visions of their trip slipping away. "I was only kidding about that. A knighted former spy is no fool. All Luke probably meant was that he hadn't actually met Freddie, but he'd heard a lot about him. It sounded as if Mrs. Frobisher really doted on him, and Sir Alfred really detested him.''

"That's probably it,'' Quent agreed to Lyndsay's relief. He glanced at his watch. "Good Lord, it's after five-thirty. I can't possibly learn enough about archaeology to sound intelligent in an hour.''

"Oh, yes, you can.'' Lyndsay gave Quent her most winning smile. "Anyone as smart as you can pick up enough in no time. Welcome to A-1 University. Ph.D.'s granted in just one hour. Sooner if you're a quick study.''

"That's right—I'll have to be Dr. Long, won't I?'' Quent said with an amused look. He took a deep breath and ran his fingers through his hair. "All right, show me what you've got.''

"I bought these books, instead of going to the library, so you can study in more detail later,'' Lyndsay said, tapping the pile on her desk corner, "and I've made a set of cram notes for you. Look these over, and then I'll show you on this map where the different things are.'' She pointed to the map spread out on her desk and then handed Quent the notes.

While he read, Lyndsay leafed through a book that was generously illustrated with photographs of various historic English buildings. A chapter headed, "Houses and Castles with Famous Ghosts,'' caught her eye. There was a picture of a shadowy shape in a dark hallway, "purported to be the ghost of Lady Cecilia, wife of the first Earl of Baskwell, who leapt to her death from the south tower after learning of the earl's death in battle.'' Lyndsay shivered involuntarily and turned the page. Poor

Lady Cecilia, she thought. Condemned to forever prowl the halls.

There were photos on the following pages of several huge houses, all claiming resident ghosts, but the one that stopped her page-turning was of a dark and gloomy-looking house with a strange Gothic-arched doorway protruding in the middle and castlelike crenellated towers at each corner. But it was not just the bizarre appearance of the house that held Lyndsay's attention. Beneath the pictures were the words, "Gravelpick Manor."

Oh, no, Lyndsay thought, glancing at Quent. If he found out that the Frobisher's house was supposed to be haunted he'd be suspicious, both of Sir Alfred and Luke. Quickly she scanned the text. Construction of Gravelpick Manor, she learned, was begun in the fourteenth century by some nameless wealthy tradesman, who completed a large, rectangular house of plain design. It passed into the hands of Secheveral Frobisher, an even wealthier and widely traveled tradesman, in the late fifteenth century. It was his idea to add the doorway and towers to go with his vision of an almost royal life-style, which he had commemorated in many large paintings of himself in elegant dress, often astride a magnificent Arabian horse. Secheveral had seven sons by a succession of wives. An ugly man, he attracted women with his wealth and power. However, one of his sons, Frederick, was extremely handsome, and when Frederick was in his teens, Secheveral found him in bed with his current wife. The article concluded, "In a rage, he drew a dagger and dispatched the young man, whose ghost still roams the southeast tower, frequently appearing—"

"I guess I've got the gist of this," Quent's voice interrupted Lyndsay's reading. "Now, what is it you wanted

to show me?'' He leaned toward Lyndsay, who started
and slammed the book shut.

"The map," she said breathlessly. "That's what I
wanted to show you. The map." Heaven forbid he should
see what she'd been reading. Unless he had a present-day
namesake, Freddie *was* a ghost! Their trip would be
called off for sure!

"That's what I thought," Quent said, looking at her
curiously. "You must have been concentrating pretty
hard on what you were reading. What did you find that's
so interesting?"

"Oh, nothing," Lyndsay replied, trying to look un-
concerned as she put the book aside. "I always concentrate like that when I'm reading about something
that . . . that takes a lot of concentration."

Quent stared at her blankly for a moment, then burst
out laughing. "I'm sorry," he said at last, "but that did
sound funny."

"That's all right," Lyndsay said, thinking it was better she sound ridiculous than for Quent to discover that
Alfred's "nephew" might have been dead for some five
hundred years! "Why don't you move around here so
you can see this map better?" she asked, indicating the
front of her desk. "Maps are hard to read sideways."

"So they are," Quent agreed. He pulled his chair
around next to Lyndsay's and bent forward to peer at the
map. "Where's North Twickham?" he asked. "Gravelpick Manor is supposed to be only a few miles south of
there."

"Uh, let's see. Right here," Lyndsay said. She leaned
over and pointed to a spot she had circled in red. As she
did so, her long dark curls brushed against Quent's
cheek. At the touch, he turned his head quickly, and

suddenly their faces were only inches apart, green eyes staring into brown.

Lyndsay had the strange sensation that time had stopped altogether, that her heart had ceased to beat, that she no longer needed to breathe. She felt as if she were in some kind of weird, suspended state generated by the current that surged between them. Her limbs seemed to be floating, disjointed from her body. Was this, she wondered, what zero gravity felt like? Could she fly around her office like a huge, wingless bird if she tried? She wanted to see if she could move, but was afraid to try for fear of breaking the spell that had come over her. Instead, she stayed motionless, noticing for the first time the ring of darker green that surrounded the translucent jade of Quent's eyes, and the way his lower lashes formed small, raylike groups, a corona beneath the eclipsing shadow of his thick, dusky lashes.

Quent seemed as mesmerized as she. His lips were slightly parted, as if he was about to speak, but he said nothing. For a long time, his eyes flicked back and forth, riveted on Lyndsay's, shifting to focus on first one and then the other. Then, very slowly, they descended to her lips. Lyndsay's heart began to pound. He would only have to move a few inches to kiss her. Or she could move. No, she didn't dare. She waited, her pulse slowing again as Quent's gaze returned to her eyes. Then, very slowly, as if by tremendous effort, he turned his head away to look at the place where Lyndsay's finger was still frozen in place.

"North of York, is it?" he said, his voice sounding strained. "Hadrian's Wall must be somewhere in the neighborhood. I have some vague recollections of reading about that long ago."

"That's . . . right here," Lyndsay said, at last moving her finger. Her own voice rang hollowly in her ears, adding to the persisting sensation that she was not yet back on firm ground. She had no idea how long they'd stared at each other. It could have been only for a second, or for several minutes. She did know something had happened to her in that time that had never happened before, and she was sure Quent had felt it, too. Even now, a supercharged envelope seemed to enclose them. They spoke of castles and priories and ancient ruins with a breathless quickness, while Lyndsay opened books to places she had marked and showed Quent the pictures she had found. He tried to appear matter-of-fact about their studies, but his eyes kept wandering back to Lyndsay's face, with a rather speculative look, she thought, and he frequently took out his handkerchief and mopped his forehead.

"Do you feel all right?" she asked after about the fifth mop. Her office was not overly warm. If anything, it was a little chilly.

"Fine. It's just a little warm in here," he replied, frowning irritably. He glanced at his watch. "I guess that's all we have time for. I hope Marian Frobisher isn't much of an archaeologist."

"I expect Sir Alfred would have mentioned it if she was, don't you?" Lyndsay asked.

"Probably," Quent agreed. He stood up. "We'd better be going. We're supposed to meet the Frobishers in the hotel lobby at seven. I wonder just how much younger Mrs. Frobisher is than Alfred. I'd hate to find out she's some dizzy showgirl he married in recent years who's only pretending to be a homebody."

"I suppose that's possible," Lyndsay said. "That might be the real reason he's worried about his nephew hanging around.'' And it would certainly fit the character of the ghostly Freddie Frobisher!

''No use speculating,'' Quent said as he slipped on his jacket. ''Let's go and find out. Remember, I'm Dr. Long now.''

''Yes, Doctor,'' Lyndsay said. ''Do I get to be Dr. Stuart? After all, I have done a lot of research.''

''I don't see why not,'' Quent replied thoughtfully. ''It makes our joint expedition seem more proper. Two colleagues on a quest for knowledge. We're probably planning to write a book together. Yes, that's it. We are. Remember that.''

''I will,'' Lyndsay said, thinking how like Quent it was to worry about the apparent propriety of their trip together. It was nice that he worried about her reputation, but she hoped he wouldn't overdo it and try to spend the entire trip addressing her as ''Dr. Stuart'' from six feet away.

IT WAS ONLY a short walk to the Frobishers' hotel. Quent spotted Alfred almost immediately, sitting on a sofa and puffing a cigar, his arm around the shoulders of a tiny woman with brightly hennaed curls that bounced like springs when she talked, which she appeared to be doing nonstop.

''She's no spring chicken,'' Lyndsay muttered when Quent pointed them out. ''Fiftyish, I'd say, wouldn't you?''

''Looks like it from here,'' Quent agreed. ''Well, are we ready, Doctor?''

''Ready,'' Lyndsay said. ''Let's dig into this case.'' She looked up, startled, as Quent made a sort of strangled sound and then burst out laughing. ''Was it that funny?'' she asked, feeling quite pleased with herself that she had made Quent laugh again. It was a lot better than having him snarl at her.

"It struck me just right," Quent replied, still grinning broadly as he took Lyndsay's arm and steered her around the furniture until they reached the Frobishers.

Sir Alfred immediately jumped to his feet, beaming at them. "Well, well, how are you two scientists this evening?" he asked. Without waiting for an answer he went on. "I'd like you to meet my wife, Marian. Marian, these are the young people I told you about, Dr. Quentin Long and Ms. Lyndsay Stuart."

"Actually, I'm a Ph.D., too," Lyndsay said, smiling at the tiny Mrs. Frobisher and holding out her hand. "Dr. Long and I collaborate on our research. I'm so happy to meet you."

"Oh, I'm just absolutely delighted Alfie found you," Marian Frobisher said, glowing at both of them and batting her obviously false eyelashes furiously as she held out both hands for a three-way handshake. "What a marvelous coincidence that you're going to my part of England. You'll love Gravelpick Manor. We'll have a simply lovely time."

"I'm sure we will," Quent replied, his smile warm and, Lyndsay thought, rather amused by the elfin Mrs. Frobisher's exaggerated vivacity. "We feel extremely fortunate that you've offered your hospitality."

The pleasantries continued while they went into the dining room and ordered dinner, Alfred insisting that the event must be celebrated with champagne. "Marian used to be on the stage, and she does like the bubbly," he remarked. "Makes her remember when she was the toast of London. No one could sing and dance like my Marian."

"Oh, now, Alfie, that was years ago," Marian protested, batting her lashes anew and simpering modestly. "Nowadays the only audience for my singing is my flowers. They do grow better with music, you know. Especially the roses." She looked back and forth between Lyndsay and Quent with a slightly defiant set to her jaw, as if expecting contradiction.

"I can certainly believe that," Lyndsay said seriously, glad Luke had warned them about the Frobishers' eccentricity. "I've heard that cows give more and better milk if they have music in their barns. I can't imagine any living thing not faring better with music in its life. Can you, Quent?" She turned to look at Quent, and could see him struggling to keep a straight face.

"No, I certainly can't," he agreed, abandoning the effort and grinning at Marian. "Unless, of course, the music consisted of my singing. In which case, instant death might be expected. Right, Lyndsay?" He threw back his head and roared with laughter, then stopped suddenly and cleared his throat, looking embarrassed.

"Uh, yes, definitely. His singing is terrible," Lyndsay replied, surprised by Quent's unusually boisterous laughter. What on earth had gotten into him? Angie's description of him as being "wound up" was putting it mildly.

"Now, Dr. Long, you just need a bit of training," Marian said, shaking a reproving finger at him. "If you have time while you're at Gravelpick Manor, I'll show you what I mean." Her eyes, bright blue and round, twinkled merrily. "I do hope you two charming young people don't plan to spend all your time working on your studies. A bit of singing and dancing is so good for the soul. Life is too short to be serious all the time. You simply must let me give a party to introduce you to the neighbors.''

''Oh, that isn't necessary,'' Quent began, then caught a glance from Alfred and added, ''but I'm sure it would be delightful. We won't be on a pressing schedule.''

''Perfect!'' Marian said, taking a healthy swallow of her champagne. ''I just love giving parties.''

She chattered on happily about her gardens, her two Pekingese dogs, Muff and Buff, and the trials of running a big old house that was constantly in need of repair, something Lyndsay could well believe after reading about it.

Lyndsay saw that Quent was trying his best to concentrate on what she said but was having difficulty. He kept watching her out of the corner of his eye, a strangely smug little smile on his face. She thought it must be the result of the combination of the champagne he had drunk and the fact that he was still short on sleep, and she resolved to keep a close eye on him when they left. She doubted he would be in any condition to drive home.

Quent did perk up when Alfred managed to get a few words in now and then, conveying the information that there was a trout stream on the premises, and extra bicycles in the barn, which were the best way of negotiating the country roads to reach the nearest sights. ''We do have an antiquity of our own that you can poke around if you like,'' he said. ''It's a strange little stone building, probably dating from the eleventh century. The walls are standing, but only part of the roof is left. It used to be on the road to North Twickham, but that road was closed off centuries ago when one of my ancestors acquired the lands on both sides of the road. Maybe you can come up with a theory about what its use was. Outside it looks like a plain little outbuilding of some kind, but inside there's a trapdoor down to a small catacomb, as if it might have been a family burial place. No skeletons, though, and no records about it anywhere. Since then it's been used for storing one thing or another." He chuckled suddenly. "I found it useful during the war for storing a certain gentleman. You'll see about that when you read my book."

"Sounds fascinating," Lyndsay said, trying to digest the fact that something had to be even older than Gravelpick Manor for Alfred to consider it an antiquity.

"Indeed it does," Quent agreed. "Just the sort of thing to add some spice to our work."

"Speaking of spice," Marian said, her eyelashes working overtime again, "Are you two—how shall I put it—involved? I mean, aside from working together?"

"Marian!" Alfred said, frowning at her. "These are serious scientists, not a pair of silly adolescents."

"I can't see that makes a bit of difference," Marian said, unperturbed. "Scientists can have a love life, too, can't they?" She arched her eyebrows toward Quent, who grinned broadly again.

"You'd better believe it," he replied much to Lyndsay's surprise.

"See, Alfie," Marian said. "They're just as human as the rest of us." She smiled innocently at Lyndsay. "I was just wondering whether to put you young people in one room or two. I know things have changed since I was a girl."

"Two rooms, please," Lyndsay said quickly, for there was a devilish spark in Quent's eyes that she had never seen before, and she was afraid that in his present state of mind his concern for propriety was about to go out the window. "We're just friends."

"Pity," Marian said, looking at them speculatively. "You do make a handsome couple."

"None of your matchmaking, Marian," Alfred said firmly. "You're apt to frighten them off."

"Yes, dear." Marian's response was the epitome of wifely meekness, but Lyndsay could tell by the gleam in her eye that she hadn't given up on her idea, which, she thought, might not be such a bad thing if she didn't push it too hard and make Quent dig in his heels. At the moment, Quent just looked amused, but she doubted he would be when he'd sobered up and had some sleep.

Both the "bubbly" and the conversation continued to flow, and it was after ten by the time Lyndsay and Quent finally parted from the Frobishers, each carrying an autographed copy of Alfred's book, *When the Clock Stopped Ticking*. To Lyndsay's relief, Quent seemed to have regained most of his normal businesslike composure, walking along with his usual purposeful stride. She had to almost struggle to keep up with him.

"What did you think of Sir Alfred?" he asked.

"He's quite an impressive man," Lyndsay replied. "It's hard to imagine anyone so good-natured and friendly being an intrepid spy. I always thought they'd be kind of quiet and reserved."

"Exactly why he was so successful, I expect," Quent said. "If he's got any major eccentricities, he's good at hiding them, too. I didn't notice anything, did you?"

"No, nothing at all," Lyndsay replied, wondering what Quent would think if he knew about the Gravelpick ghost, something that, fortunately, neither of the Frobishers had mentioned.

"I also noticed they didn't mention Freddie," Quent went on. "Must be a sore point between them."

"Must be," Lyndsay agreed. Either that or the Frobishers' eccentricity consisted of their springing old Frederick on their unsuspecting guests. "What did you think of Marian, with those wild eyelashes and her singing to her flowers?''

"I thought she was charming," Quent said. "A little eccentric, but charming." He waved Alfred's book in front of him. "If I wasn't so tired, I'd start reading this tonight. I love a good spy thriller."

"Me too," Lyndsay said. "If I didn't have to finish that Dunston report, I'd read awhile myself. Which reminds me, I have to go up to my office and get my briefcase."

"I'll come up with you." Quent said it so quickly that Lyndsay looked over at him, surprised. She was even more startled by a look so blatantly sexual that a little shiver of excitement ran through her. Good heavens, she thought, glancing quickly away. Since last night, Quent was a regular chameleon. Grouchy all day until... until that little episode in her office. Nothing had really happened then, but he had started looking at her rather strangely. Even more so at dinner. Laughing too loudly. Calm enough a few minutes ago, she had thought, but now...now he looked almost dangerous. She had wanted him to see her as a woman, but not as someone he wanted to pounce on. She decided she'd better nip this in the bud.

"Don't you think you'd better go straight home and get a good night's sleep?" she suggested, trying to sound only sweetly concerned. "You're still short on sleep, you know."

Quent shook his head and took a firm grip on her arm as they entered the building. "It's not safe here at night," he replied. "Besides, I'd like to call a cab—I'm sure my alcohol level is too high for me to be driving. And I want to take those archaeology notes home with me, as well as a couple of the books."

"But you said you were too tired to read," Lyndsay protested as he propelled her into the elevator.

"Don't argue," Quent said firmly.

"Well, you're not making much sense," Lyndsay muttered, feeling almost panicky as the elevator doors closed behind them. "I've worked late before and you weren't worried."

Quent didn't reply. To Lyndsay's relief, he did nothing but hold her arm while they soared up to the darkened offices of the A-1 Detective Agency. While she stuffed the necessary papers into her briefcase, he called a cab, then stood silently in the doorway of her office. She could feel his eyes on her but was afraid to look at him. "I have to take that one home with me so I can finish what I was reading this afternoon," she said as she added the book with the story of the Gravelpick ghost. Still without looking at him, she picked up the other three books and handed them to him. "There. All set."

"Good," he said, taking hold of her arm again as she attempted to walk past him. "Now I'll have the cab take you home first. The streets are dangerous this time of night."

Lyndsay looked up, and her heart did a skip and began thumping even harder. The gleam in Quent's eye looked far more dangerous than the streets. "I do not need a ride home," she said, frowning at him. "I can get home perfectly well on the bus. You go on home and get some sleep."

"Don't argue," he said. "I know what I'm doing."

"I wish I knew," Lyndsay said, almost running to keep up as Quent hurried toward the elevator. "I've been taking the bus for years. Why do you suddenly think you have to protect me?"

Quent pushed the elevator button and then gave her a slow, seductive smile. "I always try to protect you," he said. "I thought you'd noticed."

Lyndsay could think of no reply to that. She looked away, a strange constriction in her throat adding to her uneasiness. Somehow, things seemed to be getting out of hand, and she had no idea what to do about it.

A cab was waiting in front of the main entrance, and after helping her in, Quent climbed in beside her and gave the driver her address. While they drove, he made a few desultory comments about packing and the weather in England, but Lyndsay had little to contribute to the conversation. She was too busy wondering what to do if he paid the cabbie and decided to follow her into her apartment, then hoping she was wrong about his intentions and all he did want was to see her safely home. When they stopped in front of Lyndsay's apartment building, she turned to thank him and met that same seductive smile. For a moment, her mind went completely blank, then she managed a slightly squeaky, "Thanks for the ride."

"You're welcome," Quent said. But before Lyndsay could make any protest, he was telling the driver to wait, obviously intending to see her to her apartment door.

"You don't need to..." she began, then closed her mouth as Quent took her briefcase from her and helped her out. Through the security entrance he followed her, then up the stairs to her apartment. She unlocked her door with fingers that fumbled, then held out her hand for her briefcase. "I, uh, think I'll be safe now," she said.

The briefcase stayed in Quent's hand. "Aren't you going to invite me in for coffee?" he asked.

"But... but the cab's waiting," she stammered.

"I can go back down and send him on his way," he said. "Easy to call another one."

Good Lord, Lyndsay thought. She should offer him coffee, but would he be satisfied with that? Nevertheless she found herself saying, "I—I was just going to make some."

"Great, I could use it," he replied without hesitation.

Feeling dazed, Lyndsay turned on the lights and went inside, while he went back down and paid off the cabbie. When he returned, she waved him toward her living room. "Make yourself at home," she said. "I'll start the coffee."

"I'll watch," Quent said, following her into the kitchen.

Once again, he did nothing but stand there while Lyndsay filled the pot with water and measured out the coffee, but she could have sworn she could hear the seconds ticking by, as if a bomb were about to explode. Maybe, she thought desperately, she could pretend she wanted to change into something more comfortable and then lock herself in her room. She turned toward Quent and licked her lips nervously. "If you'll excuse me," she said, "I'd like to go and change my clothes."

Quent smiled, silvery flashes emanating from somewhere deep in the jade depths of his eyes. "Not just yet," he said. "I like that dress. You look gorgeous in red."

"I do?" Lyndsay stared at those silvery flashes, mesmerized, and then shivered as Quent put his hand out and tucked it beneath her hair, his fingers lightly tickling the back of her neck as they moved back and forth.

"Mmm-hmm," he replied, his exploring hand coming forward to catch her chin with his fingers. "All evening I kept imagining that you were like Cinderella, who would disappear in a cloud of sparkling dust when the clock struck midnight. I kept seeing the sparkles in your eyes and hair. So I had to come along and make sure it wasn't true, didn't I?''

"I—I suppose so," Lyndsay said, seeing shimmering clouds of her own dancing before her eyes as Quent's finger traced her cheek with a feathery touch. "Do you—" she swallowed over the lump in her throat "—do you want to go into the living room while the coffee perks? It's more comfortable.''

Quent looked thoughtful, then tucked an arm around Lyndsay and smiled down at her. "Let's do," he said, and walked her in to sit down beside him on the sofa. "This *is* more comfortable," he said, pulling her close.

"How about watching the late news," Lyndsay suggested, trying unsuccessfully to get up. Quent's arm held her in check effortlessly.

"Not now," Quent said, his hand creeping behind Lyndsay's neck again. His voice was low and husky as he said, "First I have to be sure you're real. If you're not, and I kiss you, you'll disappear. I have to know. Come closer."

The word "kiss" seemed to echo around and around in Lyndsay's head. Her eyes drifted to his mouth, curved into a tantalizing little smile. "Wh-what about our keeping our distance?" she croaked, feeling her self-control slipping rapidly away. "You . . . promised."

"Maybe I was wrong," he said. "Let's forget it for tonight."

"B-but . . ."

"Shh," Quent whispered, his breath warm against her lips as he turned and surrounded her with his arms. Encircled by his strength, his scent filling her nostrils, Lyndsay abandoned her fight. His lips were brushing hers now, and she was lost in a kaleidoscope of breathtaking, unreal images. Quent's eyes were huge green pools that lured her into unimaginable depths, his hands gossamer wings that carried her to unbelievable heights. The touch of his lips was soft, sweet nectar, to drink it the key to a celestial kingdom of bliss. Her eyes closed, her lips parted, and she drank hungrily, responding to Quent's increasing pressure with soft sounds of pleasure. His mouth was as magically warm and soft as before, but the currents of desire that surged through her were far beyond anything she'd ever experienced. Her fingers dug into his shoulder, then crept up to plunge into the silken thickness of his hair.

Quent's kiss deepened even more, his mouth angling back and forth against hers in delicious, sensual moves that sent Lyndsay soaring in an ecstatic dream. This couldn't be really happening, she thought. If she opened her eyes, she would find out it was only a dream. She lifted her eyelids experimentally and saw the blur of Quent's face next to hers. His eyes were partly open, filled with a dark, passionate warmth. He met her starry gaze and his eyes smiled, his arms folding even more tightly around her. Then he sighed deeply and pulled his head back a little way, still gazing at her through half-closed eyes. "You must be real," he murmured, "but you still sparkle. I wonder how you do that?"

"I don't know," Lyndsay breathed. "I see sparkles, too."

"Then it must be magic...." Quent's hand softly traced the line of her jaw, then moved between them to caress her. Through the thin fabric, the warmth of his fingers sent a rush of new electricity flying through her. She pressed against him, longing to feel his touch against her bare skin. The corners of Quent's eyes crinkled with tiny smile lines, and his mouth curved into a sleepy smile.

"Let's pretend . . . we don't have any clothes on and . . . are just about to make love," he suggested slowly, as if speaking was a great effort. "I'm . . . too tired to do anything else." With his lips still curved in a smile his eyes drifted closed and his arm closed around Lyndsay again, drawing her close. He laid his cheek against her hair and made a deep, low sound of pleasure. Then he was still.

"Quent?" Lyndsay whispered. He didn't move a muscle. He was asleep, she realized, his heavy weight pinning her against the back of the sofa.

For several minutes, Lyndsay sat there, stunned. This definitely had to be one of the strangest evenings she'd ever spent. Quent had been building up to something all day, apparently coiling tighter and tighter until, like a watch spring that suddenly fractures and gives way, he had simply passed out. Something had worn through his big-brother attitude, but she wasn't at all sure what. Was it love, or just old-fashioned lust? How could she tell? She finally decided she'd have to wait and see what he did when he was awake again and really rested. After so little sleep and quite a lot of champagne, he might have been doing things he would never normally do.

Not that she had been behaving in her usual manner, either, she thought with a belated blush. If he hadn't gone to sleep when he had, she might have willingly followed wherever he led. Luck had kept her virtuous tonight, but she wasn't sure how many similar episodes she would survive. She stroked Quent's cheek and pushed a lock of hair back from his forehead. What did he really want? she wondered. Just sex? She had something a lot more permanent in mind. Like holding him in her arms every night, laying her cheek against his hair, caressing his broad shoulders. How she wished. . . She shook her head and sighed heavily. It was no use wishing. She couldn't sit here all night. Her legs were going numb from his weight across them. Besides, she did have that blasted Dunston report to finish, a necessary evil if she was to stay in Quent's good graces as a detective.

She squirmed and wriggled free, managing to tuck a sofa pillow beneath Quent's head as he slid to one side, then struggling to lift his legs onto the sofa. That done, she covered him with a soft old quilt and tucked it around his shoulders. During her maneuvers, Quent mumbled unintelligibly, but remained sound asleep.

Lyndsay stood gazing down at him for several moments. His face looked younger in repose, his mouth softly curved, the lines around his eyes almost invisible. A lump filled her throat and her eyes grew misty. Quentin Long had become the most important thing in her present life. How she hoped he would be a part of the rest of it. "I love you, Quent," she whispered, then bent and softly kissed his cheek.

FINGERS OF LIGHT were just creeping into Lyndsay's living room when the sound of a car door slamming woke Quent. His eyes opened slowly at first, then flew open the rest of the way. *Good Lord, what have I done!* he thought, sitting bolt upright as he remembered the previous evening. What must Lyndsay think? His head throbbed and he stifled a groan and lay back down. Damned champagne. He should never touch the stuff. On top of everything else, it had been practically lethal. He was almost sure now that something was afoot among Luke, Theresa and Lyndsay, with the Frobishers part of the game. Marian Frobisher looked about as helpless as a mongoose, and she was an actress to boot. Alfred was a master of deception. Quent became determined to figure out exactly what was going on and call all their bluffs.

In the meantime, though, there was no excuse for going after Lyndsay like a stag in rut, just because she looked so gorgeous in that clingy silk dress. Poor little thing had looked terrified, at least before he'd started to kiss her. Then they'd both almost lost it. Good thing he'd passed out. But now what was he going to tell her? That he couldn't hold his liquor?

He rubbed his aching temples, then turned and buried his face in the pillows. Maybe he should pretend he didn't remember anything that had happened. The way he felt now, he wished he didn't. No, that wasn't true. He never wanted to forget the way she had felt, nestled in his arms. He had never been closer to heaven, was his last thought before he slipped back into unconsciousness. . . .

CHAPTER FOUR

LYNDSAY'S ALARM went off at six. She'd abandoned any attempt to work on the Dunston report after Quent fell asleep, finding it impossible to concentrate on pages of dull facts and figures after all that had happened. She did read the rest of the article about the Gravelpick ghost, though. Its habit, she learned, was to appear by the battlement atop the southeast tower, usually to women, apparently still obsessed by the opposite sex, a fact that Lyndsay did not find comforting. In her logical mind she knew perfectly well ghosts weren't real, but she could still remember vividly how sure she'd been as a child that she had seen the ghost of the woman murdered in that spooky old house on nearby Ell Street. Imagination, her father had said, but it hadn't convinced her racing heart, and deep inside something primitive still responded to the word "ghosts" with a shudder. She had to pretend she was back in the warmth of Quent's embrace in order to dispel the prickles of fear that the article gave her.

She bashed her alarm into silence and struggled out of bed, then put on a pair of old jeans and a sweatshirt and tiptoed in to see how Quent had survived his night on the sofa. It was, she discovered, hard to tell. He had turned so that his back was to the room, and he appeared still dead to the world, but at least she could see he was breathing. Shaking her head, Lyndsay went to brew a fresh pot of coffee and work on her report. If someone had told her yesterday that Quent would spend the night on her sofa, she'd have said they were crazy. And she was sure Quent would've agreed, at least until quite late in the evening.

She had almost finished her report when she heard a groan from the living room. Not encouraging, she thought, even though her heart did a little skip at the sound of his voice. It was not the sound of a man who was feeling his best. She got up quickly and went to him, curious to see what he might have to say for himself this morning. She found him sitting on the edge of the sofa, his head in his hands. "Good morning," she said. "Or isn't it?"

"Not very," he replied, looking up at her, bleary-eyed. "What in hell happened to me last night?"

"What do you mean, what happened?" Lyndsay asked, frowning.

"I mean, how did I end up here?" Quent asked, raising his head and shaking it like a wet spaniel dispersing water. He squinted his eyes tightly shut and rubbed his hand across them. "Oh, yeah, I remember. I brought you home in a cab and you invited me in for coffee. I must have passed out on your sofa. Sorry about that. Guess I was overtired, and champagne and I don't get along."

Lyndsay eyed him suspiciously. If he could remember her coffee invitation, which he had instigated, it seemed unlikely he couldn't remember the other things that happened before he went to sleep. What kind of game was he playing? The first time they kissed, his excuse was he'd lost control because he was so tired. Now he wanted her to believe that he didn't even remember last night's kiss because of a few glasses of champagne. Well, she was not going to let him get away with it.

"You didn't exactly wander in here and pass out," she snapped. "You fell asleep while you were kissing me. Don't tell me you can't remember that, because I don't believe it."

Quent massaged his temples with his fingers. "Yeah, I sort of remember that," he said. "Everything's pretty fuzzy, though. My head feels terrible."

"Good!" Lyndsay retorted, feeling frustrated and more than a little angry. "Why don't you come into the kitchen? I've made some coffee. I've been up since six working on that blasted report and I still have another sentence or two to finish it off." She turned and walked quickly away. Even though he didn't act like him, Quent still looked exactly like the man who had wanted to kiss her to find out if she was real. Suddenly she wanted so much to feel his arms around her again that her entire body ached, while apparently all he wanted was to forget the whole thing ever happened!

She poured him a cup of coffee, plunked a bottle of aspirin down beside it, then deliberately ignored him as he sat and watched her scribble her final words. Thank goodness she had already figured them out, she thought, or she'd never have been able to now. Quent's presence seemed to fill the space between them, and she could feel his eyes watching her as if they were actually touching her. Why was he doing that, if last night didn't matter? At last she stacked her papers into a neat pile. "There, that's done," she said. "Would you like some breakfast?" She raised her eyes to Quent, who quickly looked down at his now empty coffee cup.

"No, thanks," he said. "I'd better grab a cab on the street to take me to my car, then I'll go on home and get cleaned up for the day. Do you want me to share the cab to the office?"

Lyndsay shook her head. "No, I have several things to do here before I go. I'll take the bus."

"Okay, I'll see you later, then," Quent said, scraping his chair back and getting to his feet.

Lyndsay got up and followed him to the door. By the door he paused and looked down at her, and for a moment she thought he might have been going to say something about what had happened last night. He gave her a brief smile, but all he said was, "Thanks for your hospitality."

"Don't mention it," she said tightly.

With another "See you," he went out the door.

Lyndsay swore softly at the closed door, then turned around and gave the wall behind her a vicious kick. "Ouch!" she said, hopping on one foot and rubbing her damaged toe. That had been a stupid move, but she felt frustrated and upset enough to burst. Quent and his blasted excuses! Overtired! Champagne! She still had no idea where she really stood with him. Well, he wasn't going to get away with that again. She would make sure that the next time he kissed her he was in full possession of his faculties. And one way or another, she would definitely see there was a next time very soon!

By the time Lyndsay arrived at the office, Quent seemed to have regained his usual civil but unsmiling demeanor. It almost convinced her he wouldn't have kissed her either time if he'd really known what he was doing. His big-brother concern was back with such a vengeance that by midafternoon she was ready to throw something at him. Every few minutes he stopped by her open office door to remind her about things she did not need to be reminded about: "Don't forget your passport... Get some traveler's checks... Remember the archaeology maps...

Bring your vitamin pills... Wear loose clothes on the plane... Bring a raincoat..."

At first Lyndsay grew more annoyed each time. Then, when Angie remarked that he had acquired "the worst case of big-brother overkill" she'd ever seen, it suddenly dawned on Lyndsay that Quent was trying way too hard to make her believe nothing was different between them. She was even more suspicious when, just before she was to leave, he called her into his office and then sat and stared silently at her for several moments with a trance-like intensity.

"Have you forgotten why you wanted to see me?" she finally asked.

His eyes flew wide open, as if he had been startled out of a sound sleep by a thunderclap. "Of course not," he said. "I—I was thinking about answering this letter." He waved at an envelope on his desk.

Lyndsay went around his desk and peered over his shoulder. "Are you corresponding with the Salvation Army now?" she asked. "I think they'd rather just have a donation."

"Exactly what I plan to do," Quent said stiffly. "I simply called you in here to remind you that I'll pick you up precisely at eight tomorrow morning. Now, if you don't mind..." He flicked a glance at Lyndsay and then devoted his attention to removing the letter from the envelope.

Lyndsay sighed. Quent knew perfectly well that she knew exactly when he was picking her up, since he'd told her at least a dozen times already. He knew perfectly well that she didn't need all of those other reminders, either. Why didn't he say what he really wanted to say, whatever it was? She thought of asking him, then decided against it. This was not the time to start an argument.

Better to first get him on that plane to England. Instead, she said sweetly, "Good night, sir. I shall leave you to your voluminous correspondence. I'll try to be ready by somewhere around eight o'clock," then laughed when Quent's head jerked up and he frowned at her. "You're terribly easy to tease, do you know that?" she asked, then turned and went toward the door, feeling quite encouraged. If it was just sex Quent was after, she doubted he'd be trying so desperately to get things back the way they used to be. It was beginning to seem that Angie was right about something having gotten under his skin. Now, the question was, how to get it out into the open?

"Have a good time in England, Lyndsay," Angie said as Lyndsay passed her desk. "I sure wish I was going with you. I've never been farther east than Cleveland."

"I've never been overseas myself," Lyndsay said. "It should be an interesting experience."

"Oh, come on," Angie said with a knowing smile, "it's going to be a lot more than 'interesting' spending two weeks over there with Quent. He hasn't been hovering near your door all day just because he's afraid you'll forget your passport. I wouldn't be surprised if you two are practically engaged by the time you get back."

Lyndsay shook her head. "I don't think there's a prayer he'd move that fast, if he moves at all."

"I'll bet you lunch," Angie said.

"You're on," Lyndsay agreed.

That evening as Lyndsay packed, she speculated on what it was that made Angie so sure and why she couldn't see it herself. She did see some encouraging signs, but nothing like impending matrimony. If something really did happen, she'd have to find out what Angie's clues were. That kind of skill at reading people was worth having!

In the morning, Quent arrived promptly at eight, as Lyndsay knew he would. He looked so dramatically handsome in a new olive-green trench coat that it was all she could do to keep from trying then and there to find out how he'd respond if she flung her arms around him and kissed him when he had no excuse for not knowing what he was doing. Instead, she smiled brightly at him and said, "You look wonderful in that coat. You'd make a perfect television detective."

Quent frowned at her reprovingly. "I'm supposed to be an archaeologist, remember? Dr. Long?" he said.

"Of course I remember," Lyndsay snapped, irritated at his continuation of the previous day's endless reminders. "So am I. You'd better lay off the big-brother routine, or the Frobishers will think I'm too stupid to be one."

"Big-brother routine?" Quent raised his eyebrows.

"Yes," Lyndsay growled. "All day yesterday, nag, nag, nag. Now this morning, more of the same. I've had it up to here!" She gestured to her forehead. "Either treat me like an adult or just shut up!"

Quent looked taken aback, then smiled apologetically. "I'm sorry," he said. "I guess I *have* been overdoing it. I'll try to reform, Dr. Stuart. Shall we go?"

"I'm ready," Lyndsay replied, relieved that he had taken her fit of temper with such good humor. She had not intended to snarl at him so early in the morning, but she was darned if she was going to spend two weeks in England being treated like a child!

Quent was talkative as they drove to the airport, apparently, Lyndsay thought, almost as excited as she was. "I've been trying to imagine what Gravelpick Manor looks like," he said. "All I can come up with from some pictures I've seen of other old manor houses is something very large, probably built of some kind of stone. I wonder why Luke said it wasn't what we'd expect?''

''I can't imagine,'' Lyndsay replied, although after reading about its ghost and seeing the picture of the place, she was quite sure she knew. A mischievous thought came to her and she went on, ''I think I imagine it looking like a castle, with towers at each end and a very grand entrance.'' When he saw it, that ought to make Quent wonder if she was clairvoyant!

''I think you've read too many fairy tales,'' Quent said, giving her a tolerant smile. ''I did notice, though, that Marian made it sound more elegant than Alfred did.''

''I noticed that, too. I expect that's because Alfred is so used to it that it's just home to him. After all, his family's owned it for generations. I gathered that Marian isn't from such a privileged background.''

''That was my impression, too,'' Quent said. ''When I couldn't sleep last night, I started reading Alfred's book. He mentions meeting Marian at an after-theater party and falling in love with her at first sight, but that was a long time before they married. I'd thought maybe she was his second wife, but she isn't. I guess he didn't want to make too many plans until he was out of the spy business.''

''She waited for him for years, then?'' Lyndsay asked, wondering at the same time why Quent hadn't slept. Angie had predicted he'd be losing sleep over her, but then, it could have been excitement over the trip.

''I don't know,'' Quent said. ''He didn't mention whether she shared his early passion or even knew about it. She must have been quite young at the time. And I imagine, very pretty.''

"From looking at them together, I'd say she knew," Lyndsay said. "She looks like a one-man woman to me. It must have been terribly difficult for both of them. He couldn't really tell her why he was putting her off, could he?"

"No," Quent said, "but his cover was as a frontline correspondent for the *Times,* which would have been a reasonable excuse until the war ended. I don't know what happened later. I haven't read that far yet."

"I can hardly wait to start the book," Lyndsay said. "We'll have to take turns sitting next to Marian. I have a feeling she doesn't stop talking very often."

"Look on the bright side," Quent suggested. "You might find out her side of the story from the very beginning. Maybe there's a bestseller in that, too, and you could ghostwrite it for her."

"Ghostwrite?" Lyndsay suppressed an urge to giggle. If Quent only knew! Marian already had a ghost if she needed one. "I don't think I'd make a very good ghost," she said, "and if you're intimating that I'm supposed to do all of the listening, forget it. Marian would be terribly offended if you neglected her. All of that eyelash-batting wasn't for my benefit."

Quent sighed. "I suppose you're right. We are supposed to be grateful guests, aren't we?"

The famous eyelashes were fairly still when Lyndsay and Quent met the Frobishers at their gate at O'Hare.

"Marian's always a bit apprehensive before a flight," Alfred explained, giving his wife a comforting hug. "Don't you fret, love," he said, nuzzling her ear affectionately. "You'll have a fine time with these young people, and I'll be home before you know it."

"How many times have I heard that before," Marian said, smiling sadly. "Just don't stay any longer than two weeks."

"I won't," Alfred promised solemnly. "Two at the most."

To Lyndsay's surprise, Marian had very little to say once they boarded the plane. "I try to just eat and sleep on a long flight," she said. "It makes it go faster."

As a result, Quent had no objection to taking a turn sitting next to her. When Lyndsay stopped reading and looked back at them, they were both sound asleep. *Good,* she thought, smiling to herself. That would eliminate fatigue as an excuse for anything that happened between them after they arrived in England.

Lyndsay tried to sleep, but between Alfred's exciting book and her own anticipation of at last seeing the land of her ancestors, she did little but doze a few times before they landed at Heathrow in the very early morning. Quent still seemed a little groggy, but Marian sprang to life as if she'd been plugged into an electrical outlet as soon as her feet touched British soil.

"Grab a trolley for our bags," she instructed Quent when they reached the baggage area. "We'll be through customs and find Jepson before you can say Gravelpick Manor. Oh, I can hardly wait to get home and see my babies. They don't eat very well when their mama's away."

"Babies?" Quent asked, confused.

"I think she means Muff and Buff, her doggies," Lyndsay suggested, and Marian beamed.

"That's right. My dog children. You'll just love them—they're so cute. Almost as smart as humans, too."

"Dog children." Quent nodded and smiled vaguely. Lyndsay heard him repeat "dog children" again as he went off in the direction Marian had pointed.

"I do believe he's got a touch of jet lag," Marian said to Lyndsay with a smile. "It affects some people like that. They feel a little disoriented." Her own expression was bright. "How do you feel, dear?"

"Just fine so far," Lyndsay replied, watching Quent as he returned slowly with the trolley. He did look less alert than usual, his eyes wandering over the crowd aimlessly instead of with their usual quick, purposeful movements. Thank goodness, she thought, jet lag didn't last for long. If it did, he might try to use *that* as an excuse for anything that happened between them.

In a short time they had cleared customs and were greeted by a tall, thin regal-looking man in a chauffeur's uniform. Marian introduced him as, "Mr. Jepson, who has been with Alfred for thirty years."

Jepson doffed his cap and bowed formally, his smile revealing the most incredibly even white teeth Lyndsay had ever seen.

"His teeth look like they'd glow in the dark," Quent said, his mouth close to Lyndsay's ear as they followed Jepson and Marian.

Lyndsay giggled and grinned up at Quent, her heart doing a little flip at the mischievous lights she saw sparkling in his eyes. Had he any idea, she wondered, how devastatingly attractive he was when he discarded his usual carefully controlled demeanor? Or did he, maybe, control it just to keep hordes of women from attacking him?

Quent laughed and looked as if he was about to say something more, when suddenly his eyes widened. "Wow," he said softly.

It took Lyndsay only a split second to see what he meant. Jepson had stopped by a black limousine and was opening the back door for Marian. Alfred had told them that "their car" would meet the party at Heathrow and drive them to Gravelpick Manor, but in her wildest dreams Lyndsay had not imagined the car she now saw. It was a vintage Rolls, and every inch of its sweeping fenders and chrome headlights and bumpers shone like new. Inside, it was even more dazzling, with beautiful deep brown leather seats, and glowing, polished wood trim. Attached to the side walls in front of them were brass holders containing crystal vases, filled with fresh roses, and a console held a bottle of champagne, chilling in a vessel containing cracked ice.

"I hope you like our car," Marian said, her eyelashes resuming their spectacular antics. "It was custom-made for one of those dreadful Nazis Alfie caught. Some grateful person gave it to him as a little reward after the war."

"Nice token," Quent said, his eyes slowly sweeping the plush interior.

"Fantastic," Lyndsay said. "I've never seen anything like it." Nor had she ever seen anything like Quent's expression as he gazed around. He looked, she thought, like a child who had just discovered that Santa Claus had brought him an entire toy store. How she would love to have him look at her like that, and know that he meant it!

"Well, of course, there really isn't anything quite like it," Marian said, reaching for the champagne bottle as Jepson got the car under way. "Would you mind?" she said sweetly, handing it to Quent. "I'm always afraid I'll shoot someone in the eye if I try to open one."

Quent took the bottle and eyed it thoughtfully for a moment, then held it up as if sighting along a gun barrel. "It'd make an interesting weapon," he said. "Imagine a war fought with champagne corks. If you missed you'd have to empty the bottle and use it as a club." He gave Lyndsay a rather silly grin. "That would be an archaeological find, wouldn't it? A whole battlefield of nothing but skeletons and champagne bottles? I wonder which side would win. The straightest shooters or the fastest drinkers?"

Marian laughed delightedly. "What fun! I'm so glad you're not one of those stuffy professors who's so serious he can't make a joke. They're so deadly dull. He must be wonderful to work with," she added, turning to Lyndsay.

"Absolutely marvelous," Lyndsay agreed, doing her own subdued version of eyelash-batting in Quent's direction. "I just never know what clever idea he's going to come up with next."

Quent smiled but said nothing, his attention now devoted to removing the wire from the champagne cork. "Better have a glass ready," he said as he began pressing the cork upward with his thumbs.

Marian opened a door beneath the ice bin and took a crystal champagne glass from the little cabinet. "You're closer," she said, handing the first glass to Lyndsay and then getting out two more.

The cork slowly moved upward. Lyndsay held her breath, hoping Quent wouldn't blast a hole in the car roof with it, but he succeeded in edging it out perfectly, so that not even a drop of champagne was lost.

"Very professional," Marian complimented him as he filled the glasses.

Lyndsay threw Quent a look as he took his glass. Had he forgotten what the champagne had done to him only a day and a half before? Or was he going to be happy for an excuse to kiss her again? She shivered.

"Years of experience," Quent was saying. "Very much like removing the stopper from a flask of fermented coconut milk, the favorite drink of the natives of Mora-Mora."

"How fascinating," Marian said. "I'm not sure I've heard of Mora-Mora. Where is it?"

"The South Pacific. Near Bora Bora." He leaned across Lyndsay and added confidentially, "Much more interesting place, though. Much more interesting."

Lyndsay almost choked on her first sip of champagne, but she managed to confine her distress to a few little coughs, while all the while Quent went on to regale Marian with details of his time with the fictitious Mora-Morans. Was it jet lag that had set his imagination into overdrive, she wondered, or was it deliberate? It certainly wasn't the champagne, for he had yet to take his first sip. Whatever it was, she hoped they didn't soon meet someone who was a whiz at geography, or who wondered how Quent happened to specialize in what appeared to be a strange combination of archaeology and cultural anthropology. Marian, however, was not that person. She was completely enthralled with his story.

"Isn't that right, Dr. Stuart?" Quent's voice shook Lyndsay out of her speculative trance.

"I'm sorry," she said, "I wasn't listening. What was it you said?"

"Never mind. I know you've heard my story so often that it's boring," Quent replied, his smile teasing, but his eyes displaying that same aggressively sensual look they'd had the night he took her home. "Why don't you tell

Marian about that perfectly preserved man you found encased in a block of ice in northern Siberia?''

Lyndsay stared at him, feeling close to panic. She was usually quite imaginative, but being called upon so suddenly to come up with a story while at the same time her heart had started pounding in an automatic response to that gleam in Quent's eyes left her mind a complete blank. "Well, I, uh, that is…it was very cold, there," she began. She looked at Quent pleadingly, but all she got in return were some mirthful silver flashes from sparkling green eyes, which then focused on her lips and stayed there. Her cheeks began to feel hot. She turned her head away, looking at Marian, instead. "I didn't really do it. There were a lot of people there besides me," she said lamely.

"But what an exciting find!" Marian said enthusiastically. "I think I remember seeing pictures of that in a science magazine. Wouldn't it be something if you could have brought him back to life? Cryogenics. Isn't that what they call freezing people like that today so they can bring them back later?"

"Yes. I think so," Lyndsay said, relieved that Marian had wandered onto another topic. "Will it work? I wonder."

Her question generated a lively discussion. For a while, Lyndsay took part, but by the time her glass of champagne was empty her eyelids were feeling very heavy. It was almost as if those bright, intense looks from Quent were drawing her to him, sapping all her energy. His deep voice seemed to come in waves that washed over her, while the rhythmic purring of the Rolls engine played a soothing counterpoint. She should have slept on the plane, she thought as her eyes drifted closed. She hated to miss anything, but . . .

She felt someone take the glass from her fingers. They rounded a corner and she started to slide sideways, stopped by a smooth, hard object she recognized as Quent's shoulder. As if from a great distance she heard Marian say softly, "Quent, put your arm around her so she doesn't slide back and forth. There are a lot of turns up this way and these leather seats are slippery." At that, Lyndsay's mind woke up enough to allow her to open her eyes if she wanted to, but it also woke up enough to allow her to realize now was not the time to do so, not if she wanted to encourage Marian's attempts to play matchmaker. Did she? She decided that she did. Marian would have romance and love in mind, presumably followed by marriage. Quent might well need encouraging along those lines.

She kept leaning limply against Quent and soon felt his arm slip behind and around her, making her feel warm and secure. It was, she decided, the nicest place in the world to be. Pretending she was moving in her sleep, she pressed herself closer and leaned her head against his chest and drifted into a real sleep.

Quent smiled at Marian, who was beaming at him benignly. "She must be tired," he said. "She didn't sleep much on the plane."

"She's a dear," Marian said. "So pretty, too."

"And an excellent scientist," Quent said. He put down his half-empty glass, adjusted his arm to pull Lyndsay even closer, then leaned his head back against the cushions and closed his eyes. "I believe I'll take another nap, too," he said.

He doubted he'd actually sleep. It was too pleasant, having Lyndsay close to him again. He expected Marian would try to arrange plenty of opportunities for him to do exactly that in the next couple of weeks, for he was certain now that Luke had cooked up this whole scheme. Clever of Luke to have Marian be such an obvious matchmaker that Quent wouldn't notice whatever else had been planned. It was going to be very interesting to see what it was, and even more interesting to see the reaction when he called everyone's bluff. The only hard part might be to keep pretending he didn't suspect a thing. Should he appear to be falling for it, or should he act the reluctant lover? Probably the latter, if they were going to allow their whole plot to spin out. That wouldn't be easy, either. He was growing surer every day that Lyndsay was the woman for him.

CHAPTER FIVE

LYNDSAY WAS still asleep when they reached Gravelpick Manor, and Marian's happy chirrup, "We're home, dears," wakened her. She gathered that Quent had dozed off, too, for when she looked up at him he was blinking sleepily and seemed surprised to see her face so close to his.

"Well, here we are," she said, smiling at him as Jepson opened the door and cool, damp early morning air rushed in.

"Uh, yes, so we are," he said, frowning uncomfortably and extricating his arm from behind her as she leaned forward to follow Marian.

His response was disappointing, but Lyndsay had no time to brood about it in the hubbub that greeted their arrival. As soon as Marian stepped out of the limousine, her two Pekingeses came bounding out of the door and down the steps of the house, leaping and bounding around her as she picked up each one and hugged and kissed it.

"Oh, you darlings," she said, scrunching up her nose at their wet kisses. "It's so good to be home. Hello, Whitby. Hello, Sofia."

Her second greetings were for the two people who had followed the dogs down the steps. One was a tall, cadaverous-looking man in a black suit with a few threads of yellowish gray hair combed across his bald head, the other a short, black-haired woman wearing a white apron over a black dress. She was as round as the man was scrawny, but her plumpness did not, Lyndsay noticed, give her an especially pleasant appearance. Her hair was drawn tightly back in a bun, and her thin lips were pursed into a straight, uncompromising line. All in all, the pair were perfectly matched to the forbidding-looking stone house behind them, which was exactly as it appeared in the photo she'd seen, but was almost twice as large as she'd anticipated. She was staring at it, thinking apprehensively that it looked like a perfect home for ghosts and vampires, when Quent's voice, close to her ear, made her start visibly.

"How did you know what it would look like?" he demanded in low tones. "Good Lord, you're jumpy. What's the matter?"

"I imagined it would be sort of castlelike, but I didn't think it'd resemble a set for *The Bride of Frankenstein.*" Lyndsay whispered back. She glanced at the two servants. "They look like part of the cast."

"Mmm. I see what you mean," Quent said. There was a great deal of gesticulating going on, especially on the part of the woman, and Marian was nibbling one of her fingernails pensively. "Seems to be some kind of problem. Maybe we should see if we can help." He moved to Marian's side with Lyndsay right behind him. "Is something wrong?" he asked.

"The clock is missing," pronounced the tall servant in scratchy, dour tones.

"*The* clock?" Quent raised his eyebrows questioningly at Marian.

"Our old mantel clock from the library," Marian explained. "It was given to one of Alfred's ancestors by an emperor of China. Of course, it's very unusual and extremely valuable, but what worries Whitby and Sofia more is that there was no sign of anyone breaking into the house. Someone apparently got in without triggering the alarm system. Oh, by the way, Whitby is our butler and family retainer, and Sofia is our housekeeper.''

Marian introduced them to the pair as famous archaeologists Dr. Quentin Long and Dr. Lyndsay Stuart. Whitby bared yellowed teeth in what Lyndsay assumed was a smile, and Sofia gave a perfunctory nod.

''Is there a reason for someone to want that particular clock?'' Quent asked, looking around the little group. ''I'm guessing it'd be difficult to sell if it's so unusual.''

''Exactly, sir,'' said Whitby. ''It's not a logical theft. One might assume the thief was simply too stupid to think of that, but he's a clever rascal otherwise. The doors were securely locked, and the alarm system was still functioning this morning.''

''The clock was there last night?'' Lyndsay asked.

''Oh, yes, Dr. Stuart,'' Sofia replied in a cool, slightly accented voice. ''It strikes the hour, and I heard it strike just as I was retiring.''

''It's a regular mystery, isn't it?'' Marian said. ''Oh, dear. I do wish Alfred were here. I suppose I'll have to report it to Constable Barnwell, in case the clock turns up in North Twickham, but I do hate to have him poking around the place. He's a nice old fellow, but I doubt he'd recognize an ax murderer if he caught him with his weapon in hand.''

''Perhaps Dr. Long can help. He's quite a good amateur detective,'' Lyndsay said, giving Quent an encouraging smile. ''Isn't that right, Quent?''

''Well, yes, but...'' Quent said, looking so embarrassed that Lyndsay wondered what had become of the imagination that had invented Mora Mora so quickly. He had been so creative in the car that she had assumed he would easily be able to invent an explanation for his skill at detective work. Instead, he rubbed his forehead thoughtfully, apparently stalling for time.

"He's too modest," Lyndsay said, deciding to jump into the breach. "He worked for a detective agency in the summers he was in college. He's often said it was a great help when he had to solve some mystery about an early culture." She glanced at Quent to see whether he would pick up this cue or remain silent. She was relieved when he nodded, now seeming to have gotten his act together.

"That's quite true," he said. "There are many similarities between detective work and archaeological exploration. One has to know the right questions to ask in both cases."

Marian smiled delightedly. "I can see how that might be true. Tell me, Quent, what questions should we be asking right now?"

Lyndsay almost burst out laughing at the serious, thoughtful way Quent appeared to be pondering that question, for she was sure that dozens of ideas had already popped into his fertile detective's mind. That part of his brain never seemed to take any time off. At last he cleared his throat and said, "It's a very large house. Is there any chance someone could have come in during the day and stayed hidden until everyone was asleep before he took the clock?"

"Oh, no, sir," Whitby said quickly. "Definitely not. Sir Alfred took that eventuality into account when he designed the security system. One has to punch some numbered buttons in the correct order if he wishes to leave after the system is set for the night. It sets itself automatically, at precisely ten o'clock."

"Hmm." Quent shook his head. "This is a stumper, isn't it? I'm afraid I'll have to think about it for a while."

"Please, don't bother," Marian said. "That silly old clock isn't worth it. It's turned me into a terrible hostess. Here we are, worrying over that when we should be going in for some breakfast. After that, Sofia will show you to your rooms and you can change into something more comfortable. You might explore the house and the grounds, or bicycle around wherever you want. I'll be busy inspecting my gardens for most of the day. I've been gone for so long, there's no telling what kind of pests and blights may have gotten into them."

Marian swept up the steps and into the entrance hall. "Terribly large, isn't it?" she said, seeing Lyndsay's dazed expression. "I sometimes use it for a ballroom." She whirled around once and then hurried on so fast that Lyndsay could only gain a quick impression of acres of dark, polished wood and a huge, spiral staircase with a bloodred carpet running up the middle. Marian started down a dark paneled hallway to the right of the staircase. "I call this Ancestor Row," she said, gesturing to the numerous paintings of men and women, old and young, that hung on the walls. She paused and pointed a red-laquered fingertip at a picture of a handsome young man with long black hair and eerily penetrating dark eyes. "You may have heard of the Gravelpick ghost," she said. "That's him. The original Frederick Frobisher."

"Original?" Quent asked. Lyndsay felt her heart lurch in her chest.

"The first one," Marian said. "There have been several since the fifteenth century, including Alfred's present nephew. He's a delightful young man. I'll have to be sure he comes up from London while you're here."

Lyndsay felt limp with relief. So there was a real, live Frederick Frobisher. However, Marian's casual reference to the ghost was not encouraging. "Do you, uh, see the ghost often?" she asked in a squeaky voice.

Marian looked at her quickly. "Oh, no, dear, of course not," she said comfortingly. "In fact, I've never seen him in all the years I've lived here." She laughed lightly. "I guess he doesn't care for redheads, since that's what got him into trouble in the first place." Seeing Quent's questioning look, she went on to explain the story, while Lyndsay wondered nervously how the original Frederick felt about brunettes. Quent listened politely, but Lyndsay could tell by the look on his face that he gave no credence to the ghostly Freddie's reappearance.

Marian led them down the rest of the long hallway. "Here we are," she said, as they entered a room at the back of the house. "This is the breakfast room. It's my favorite room at Gravelpick. I hope you like it, even though it's not in keeping with the historical period of the rest of the house. Some purists seem to take offense at that."

"I certainly don't. I think it's lovely," Lyndsay said, gazing around in both surprise and relief. The rest of the house had seemed oppressively dark, but the breakfast room, situated in a glass-enclosed bay overlooking a green lawn edged with red geraniums, was light and airy. The walls were covered in floral-printed silk, the carpet was jade green, the table and chairs ivory. Large ferns in colorful ceramic pots were placed on either side of the windows and doors. "Isn't it, Quent?" she prompted, as he looked about with what she called his "vacuum eyes," habitually registering every detail for future use on a case.

"Yes, it is," he agreed, giving Lyndsay a glance that told her he was not pleased at her prompting him. "It's very attractive. It must look like spring in here all year-round."

"What a charming thing to say," Marian said, beaming at Quent. "That's exactly the effect I tried to achieve. The rest of the house is so dark and dreary that I had to have someplace to escape it. Alfie won't hear of changing the rest, but I fussed and carried on and used every trick I knew until he gave in on this room." She smiled at Lyndsay conspiratorially. "We girls do have our little bag of tricks, don't we?"

Lyndsay wasn't sure quite how to answer that one, so she smiled vaguely and nodded.

Quent, obviously operating in his detective mode, began asking questions as soon as they sat down to eat. "How many rooms are there in Gravelpick Manor?" was his first.

"Oh, goodness, that depends on how you count," Marian answered. "If you count the entrance hall and the upstairs hall and the towers and all of the servants' rooms, most of which aren't used any more because we have day help, there are about fifty. We only use twenty or so regularly."

"Twenty or so," Quent echoed thoughtfully, and Lyndsay figured he was probably thinking that left thirty rooms where someone could hide for heaven knew how long in this immense house. His face, which had assumed its usual A-1 Detective Agency sobriety, did not reveal anything except casual interest. As they ate a hearty breakfast, he managed to innocuously slip in several questions about the number of servants, what they did and where they lived all under the guise of curiosity about how a person managed a house as large as Gravelpick Manor. All he found out, though, was that Marian had little interest in such details.

"Sofia manages all the domestic help," Marian told him. "I don't know what I'd do without her. She knows more about that than I do."

After breakfast, Sofia led Lyndsay and Quent up the stairs to their rooms. At the top of the stairs was a larger-than-life painting of a black-haired man on a white horse. The man's clothing was velvet, richly adorned with gold, his horse magnificent in trappings of ornate silver, but the artist had made no attempt to conceal the man's bulbous nose or anthropoid brow ridge. That, Lyndsay thought, must be the infamous Secheveral Frobisher. He was ugly indeed.

The upstairs hallway was long, and Lyndsay had lost count of the number of doors they had passed by the time Sofia stopped only two doors from where the hall ended at a heavy arched door, chained and padlocked shut.

"We don't go into the towers," Sofia said unnecessarily, gesturing toward the door. "The stairs are unsafe."

Not to mention the fact, Lyndsay thought, that the ghost was supposed to inhabit one of them. Her book had said the southeast tower, but she had not yet gotten her directions straight. She hoped that it wasn't the one so close to her bedroom.

"This will be your room, sir," Sofia said, opening the second door from the tower. "Would you like me to send someone to help you unpack?"

"No, thank you," Quent said. "I can manage that myself."

The housekeeper raised her eyebrows slightly. "Very well. How long will you be staying?"

"About two weeks," Quent replied.

This time the woman pursed her lips before she said, "Then you'll need laundry done. I'll have one of the maids bring you a basket." She turned and bustled to the next door and repeated her question about unpacking to Lyndsay.

"No, thank you," Lyndsay said, although she could tell Sofia found her response wanting. Probably, she thought, a sign to Sofia that these Americans weren't used to living in such a grand style.

"Very well," the housekeeper replied again. "If you need any assistance dressing, you can call the maid by pressing this button." She showed Lyndsay a small button next to the door frame.

"Thank you," Lyndsay said. Never in her life had she had a maid assist her in dressing, but she might take advantage of the service just for the novelty of it. Sofia nodded and Lyndsay stepped into her room. Seconds later, she heard a door shut somewhere nearby in the hallway and peeked out again. Sofia had disappeared. There must be a servants' staircase behind one of those doors, Lyndsay thought, before she went on into her room, closing the door behind her.

The room was large and high ceilinged, with tall, narrow windows and heavy, dark red brocaded draperies. The carpet and bedcover were the same dark color, the furniture massive. Lyndsay's suitcases had been placed next to an armoire that looked big enough to hold a small car. The only bright spots in the room were a beautiful crystal chandelier in the center of the ceiling and the white sash curtains at an open window, billowing in the breeze.

"It still looks like *The Bride of Frankenstein* to me," Lyndsay muttered as she crossed to the windows. "I wonder what you can see from up here?" She pushed the sash curtains aside, leaned on the window ledge and looked out.

The view was breathtaking. To her left, she could see not only the same green lawn visible from the breakfast room, but also, beyond it, a small willows shaded pond reflecting the blue of the sky, and a road bordered by stone fences that meandered between a series of rolling hills sliced into irregularly shaped fields by hedgerows. Just below her window were Marian's precious gardens, and Marian and her dogs were there, conferring with a bent little man holding a hoe. To the right, the view of more lawn and a woods beyond was partially obscured by the tower. Lyndsay leaned out farther and looked up at the tower. What a fantastic view there must have been from the top, she thought. It rose a good ten feet above the corner of the house. There were no windows, only a few small openings below the battlement, just like towers designed to defend a real castle.

She squinted at the battlement silhouetted against the blue sky and morning sun, trying to imagine flags flying and men in medieval dress letting loose their arrows on attackers below. A faint movement caught her eye and she scanned the rim of the tower. Suddenly she gasped. Her heart did a flip inside her chest and then started to race. A face, that of a handsome young man with long, coal-black hair, had appeared in one of the notches of the battlement, and as she stared at it, transfixed, he seemed to smile at her wistfully, then gradually faded away. It was the ghost of Frederick Frobisher! she thought.

Trembling uncontrollably, Lyndsay pulled back into her room. "Quent!" she shrieked, stumbling toward her door, on legs that seemed to belong to someone else. "Quent!" she shrieked again.

"What is it?" Quent, bare-chested, burst through her door at the same moment Lyndsay arrived there. She flung herself blindly toward him and he caught her, folding his arms around her and patting her back comfortingly as he said, "Good Lord, Lyndsay, what's wrong? Did you see the ghost already?'' He pulled his head back and gave her a quirky little smile.

Lyndsay realized in a flash that Quent would think she was a mental case if she told him she had. He would expect a stalwart detective to pooh-pooh its existence, just as he did.

''Oh, goodness no, nothing like that,'' she croaked, trying to get her nerves under control. Quent's bare-chested closeness was undermining her efforts almost as fast as she could make them. ''I—I can't get my suitcase open,'' she blurted finally, then wondered why on earth she had said something that stupid as Quent released a breath and shook his head.

''I thought someone was trying to kill you,'' he said. He let go of Lyndsay and strode to her suitcase, sitting on a rack next to the armoire. He tried one of the catches, then turned his head and frowned. ''No wonder you can't open it,'' he said. ''It's locked.''

''Oh, goodness, silly me,'' Lyndsay said, smiling weakly. ''I usually don't remember to lock it, and then when I do I can't remember that I did.''

Below Quent's frown, his lips twitched, but his voice was stern as he said, ''Get the key. Or did you forget it? Is that why you panicked?''

''No, of course not. It's on my key ring.'' Lyndsay dug her key ring out of her purse and put it into Quent's outstretched hand. ''It's the tiny one.''

''I know,'' Quent said dryly. He quickly unlocked the catches and opened the suitcase. ''There you are,'' he said, handing the keys back to Lyndsay. ''Any other dire emergencies I can help you with?''

''No, I guess not. Thank you,'' Lyndsay said. Except the one that seeing him half-naked was creating inside of her. She felt as if she were about to catch on fire.

"Next time try knocking on my door," Quent said.

Lyndsay could tell by the tone of his voice and the sly twinkle in his eyes that he was laughing at her. Well, she might have sounded not quite bright to him, but it was the best she could do under the circumstances. "I'll remember," she said meekly. "I'm sorry I was such a dummy."

Her eyes wandered downward, taking in the smattering of dusky hair on Quent's chest that trailed off in a little V above his navel. His skin was tanned and smooth against his firm muscles, and her palms itched to touch him. She clenched her fists and resolutely raised her eyes back to his. What she saw there sent a shock wave through her even greater than the sight of the ghostly face on the tower. His eyes, their centers dark and burning bright, were looking at her with a desire so intense that it made her tremble. Mesmerized, she watched as he reached out and touched her hair, his eyes first following his hand, then moving slowly back to meet hers. She held very still as he stroked her hair gently, then pulled his hand back.

"Are you all right now?" he asked.

"Yes, I'm fine," she replied. If being fine was wanting so much for him to give up fighting it and kiss her that she felt as if every neuron in her body was firing at once.

"This is a rather forbidding old place, isn't it?" he said.

Lyndsay nodded. "Very." She gestured at the armoire. "That looks like the kind of thing bodies fall out of when you open it."

Quent smiled. "So that's it. I knew something had frightened you. Don't be ashamed to tell me something like that. You can't help having a vivid imagination any

more than you can help—'' he paused for a fraction of a
second, apparently in some conflict over what he was
about to say, then concluded ''—being beautiful.''

Lyndsay could scarcely believe what she had heard.
Quent thought she was beautiful! A rush of emotion sent
tears to her eyes. ''Thank you,'' she whispered. ''That's
the nicest thing anyone's ever said to me.''

''It's just the truth,'' Quent said, looking embarrassed, as if, Lyndsay thought, he couldn't quite believe
he had said it himself. ''Would you like me to open that,
uh, thing for you?''

''Would you?'' Lyndsay said. The moment had slipped
away, but it had left behind a warm, wonderful feeling.
Quent was in completely normal condition, no fatigue or
champagne or any noticeable jet lag to excuse what she
had seen in his eyes or heard from his lips. Those words,
combined with the fact that he hadn't taken advantage of
the situation to kiss her might even be a sign that his
feelings did run deeper than pure physical attraction.

''There you are. Not a body in sight,'' Quent said,
flinging open the doors of the armoire.

''Thank goodness,'' Lyndsay said. ''Now I can unpack.''

''And I can finish unpacking,'' Quent said. He started
for the door, then stopped and turned back. ''When
you've finished unpacking, put on something warm and
comfortable so we can go bicycle riding a little later, and
then go down and talk to Whitby and Sofia and find out
what you can about the other servants. See if there are
any new ones, if anyone's had financial problems lately—
that sort of thing. The clock theft may have been an inside job.''

''But you said yourself it would be hard to sell,''
Lyndsay said, wishing he would forget about the clock

and concentrate on her being beautiful instead. Why did that stupid clock have to be stolen just now?

"Hard, but not impossible," Quent said. "There's a market for almost anything rare and valuable if you know where to look."

"Maybe the butler did it," Lyndsay suggested dryly. Quent ignored her.

"I think I'll go outside and begin to get the lay of the land," he went on. "I also thought I'd see what outside employees they have. It must take quite a few to keep up this place and manage the farm."

"You're starting to sound a little too much like a professional detective," Lyndsay said, frowning. "You'd better be careful, or Marian will get suspicious."

Quent shook his head. "We won't push it too hard, but I don't think Marian has a suspicious bone in her body. I can see why Alfred's worried about her. He'd want us to investigate."

"I suppose you're right," Lyndsay said with a sigh. "What's your room like?"

"A museum. Carved lions all over the place." Quent glanced at his watch. "I'll meet you out in front in about an hour, and we can try out the bicycles before lunch. We should probably get in condition before we try riding very far. I haven't been on a bike in years."

"Neither have I. That's a good idea," Lyndsay said.

Quent nodded. "I'll see you in an hour, then."

HE WENT BACK to his room and made an additional note on a pad of paper where he had already written: "1. L knew how Gravelpick looks! 2. Missing clock? 3. Ghost so L can act scared. 4. L's room next to ghost tower." To those he now added, "5. Lyndsay denies ghost??" Maybe, he thought as he dressed, she was embarrassed to use it, but that didn't seem right, either. That was no act. Something had really frightened her. If it happened again, he would question her more thoroughly. No one had a right to scare her that badly, no matter how good their intentions. Besides, seeing her like that had almost been too much for him. Her eyes had been so huge and dark. He couldn't help telling her she was beautiful. He would have liked to do a lot more than just tell her....

CHAPTER SIX

WHEN QUENT LEFT, Lyndsay closed the door behind him and made a terrible face. If she could catch the idiot who stole the clock, she'd throw him or her across the room and then jump on him. She had no desire to spend an hour interrogating people who probably knew no more about where the clock had gone than she did. Bicycle riding sounded more promising, if Quent could get his mind off that blasted clock. It would be a real blessing if this Constable Barnwell surprised Marian and found the darned old thing.

Quickly, Lyndsay hung her dresses on the rod in the armoire and tucked her lingerie and other folded clothes into the drawers. As she changed into the casual clothes Quent had prescribed, she looked toward the open window and smiled wryly. At least old Frederick the First had helped her to get Quent's mind off his detective work for a little while. How did the ghost know to appear at the battlement just then? Or did he hang around there all the time? She had never heard of a ghost that came out in the daytime, in full color. . . .

"Wait a minute," Lyndsay muttered, pausing with hairbrush in hand. Luke Thorndike was involved in their visit, and the present Freddie was supposed to be a genius at electronics. Could that "ghost" have been something they'd cooked up? She thought for a minute, then shook her head. There wouldn't be any way they could tell when and if she would look up at the tower. But if it wasn't them . . .

Trying not to think about that possibility, Lyndsay hurriedly finished brushing her hair, picked up her windbreaker and left the room. As she entered the hallway, she paused and looked toward the tower door. Certainly no one could get through that from the other side without beating it down with an ax. Of course, ghosts didn't worry about such obstacles. . . . She shivered involuntarily, then took a deep breath. "Ghosts are not real," she told herself firmly. Quent was right. She had a vivid imagination. It was time she turned it off and got her mind on what Quent had told her to do, instead of a lot of nonsense.

She made herself refrain from looking over her shoulder by counting the number of doors she passed before she reached the stairs. There were eight, and on the walls between, seven dark old pictures in heavy gilt frames that looked as if they could well be by some of the Old Masters. No wonder Alfred had installed an elaborate security system! Maybe whoever took the clock was testing his ability to get in and out undetected, and planned to come back for something even more valuable. Funny, but just from meeting Alfred Frobisher she never would have pegged him for a man of such immense wealth.

Downstairs in the entrance hall, Lyndsay paused again. Where might Sofia be? She could wander around for hours and never find her. She peered into one room at the front of the house and discovered the formal dining room. A table of gleaming cherry wood that looked as if it would easily seat thirty people stood in the middle beneath a pair of spectacular chandeliers, rows of chairs stood in stiff rows along the walls, but there was no one in sight. She had turned toward the stairs again when she heard voices coming from the back of the house. Following the sound, she reached the door of the library, from where the clock had disappeared. She saw Sofia talking to a young blond woman in a maid's uniform, black with a white apron and a perky white triangular cap.

"Yes, ma'am, it was here yesterday morning when I dusted," the young woman was saying.

"Did you find any clues?" Lyndsay asked, making her presence known.

"I'm afraid not, Dr. Stuart," Sofia said with a brisk shake of her head. "Tessie here says everything was just as usual in the morning."

"It must be a very loud clock," Lyndsay said thoughtfully. "I remember you heard it when you went to bed, and this is such a big house."

Tessie grimaced. "It's the loudest. There's a little man that pops out and bangs a gong. If you've got your back to it and the darned thing goes off, it nearly scares the life out of you. I'm just as glad it's gone. I always thought it was ugly, too, with those carved snakes and weird faces all over. Just an ugly old dust catcher, I'd call it."

"Tessie!" Sofia said severely, but Tessie only grinned and walked away, swinging her feather duster in her hand. Sofia looked after her and shook her head again. "It's fortunate she's a good worker," she said darkly when the girl was gone. She turned her frown on Lyndsay. "Can I help you with something, Dr. Stuart?"

"Perhaps," Lyndsay replied. "Dr. Long's got me helping him play detective, looking for clues. Was there anyone at all in here yesterday besides the staff?"

"Not a soul, Dr. Stuart," Sofia replied. "It's completely baffling, isn't it?"

"Certainly appears to be," Lyndsay agreed. She asked the questions Quent had recommended, but Sofia had nothing helpful to offer. None of the servants was new, and as far as she knew, all were law-abiding citizens. She did not, she told Lyndsay somewhat stiffly, pry into their personal lives.

"My only concern is that they do their work well," she said.

"I imagine seeing to that must take all your time," Lyndsay said, smiling sympathetically in hopes of breaking through Sofia's icy demeanor.

"It does," Sofia replied without any sign of thawing. "Now, if you'll excuse me?"

"Certainly," Lyndsay said, and Sofia bustled off. She glanced around the huge, high-ceilinged room with its floor-to-ceiling bookshelves filling every wall, leaving room only for the fireplace at one end and a large bay window overlooking a garden. It was a more pleasant room than the others, except for Marian's breakfast room. In the center was a long table with a large world globe in the middle and, looking rather out of place, a television set facing the fireplace wall. On either side of the fireplace were comfortable, well-used lounge chairs with reading lights beside them. A favorite spot for the Frobishers to spend an evening, she guessed.

Lyndsay went back to the entrance foyer and peered into the room that ran along the front of the house, opposite the foyer from the dining room and parallel to the library. It was, she decided as she stared into it in awe, what would be called a grand salon with a capital *G*. Take the furniture out, and Secheveral could have played polo in there! A modern family could set up a basketball court. She was smiling to herself, imagining the ancient room full of noisy, rollicking children, when a raspy voice behind her nearly startled her out of her skin.

"You wished to see me?"

Lyndsay gasped and whirled around. "Oh, Whitby! It's you," she said. "I didn't hear your footsteps."

"Sorry to startle you, Dr. Stuart," Whitby said, his face crinkling into an apologetic smile. "Sofia said you were questioning the servants about the missing clock."

"Just looking for clues," Lyndsay said, smiling back at the elderly man. At least he appeared friendlier than Sofia. "I'm afraid Dr. Long is taking his detective work a little too seriously. He wanted me to ask if you'd seen anything or anyone unusual yesterday."

Whitby shook his head. "No, I certainly didn't. There is one person, though..." He paused, looking distressed.

"Go on," Lyndsay encouraged.

"It's Sir Alfred's nephew, Frederick. Sir Alfred and his nephew are not...on the best of terms at the present time. It's possible that Master Frederick breached the security system and then took the clock just to prove he could and cause an uproar."

"I gathered from some things Sir Alfred said before we left him that his nephew is good at electronics," Lyndsay said. "Are you saying he's good enough to disable the security system?"

Whitby looked uncomfortable again. "It wouldn't be the first time," he said. "He seems to delight in distressing his uncle. Please, Dr. Stuart, don't breathe a word of what I've said to madam. She...she is very fond of the young man."

"Of course not," Lyndsay said quickly. "Do you think Freddie will come around and bring the clock back now that Mrs. Frobisher is home?"

"I shouldn't be at all surprised," Whitby replied.

Lyndsay nodded. "I'll pass along what you said to Dr. Long. Perhaps he shouldn't take the robbery too seriously, and he should wait and have a talk with Freddie."

"I'd recommend that," Whitby said. "There are so many other things around the manor that would be more reasonable for a thief to take. Silver and gold. Easy to dispose of for money."

"I'll mention that to Dr. Long, too," Lyndsay said. "Thank you, Whitby. You've been very helpful. I think I'll go and see if I can find Dr. Long now. He said he was going outside to look around."

Whitby opened the front door for Lyndsay, bowing gravely as she passed. He was, she decided, one of the nicer features of Gravelpick Manor. It wouldn't take long to get used to being treated like royalty.

She had just reached the bottom of the outside stairs when she spotted Quent coming back up the road toward the house. For several minutes she stood still and watched him, a twinge of longing tugging at her heart. With his erect bearing and long stride, he looked as if he could be the lord of this estate. The burnished gold of his hair and the dark gold of the turtleneck sweater he wore added to his regal appearance. Almost any woman, Lyndsay thought with a sigh, would think he looked like a perfect romantic hero. How wonderful it would be if she could run to him and fling her arms around him, and he would welcome her with a kiss. She sighed again. Maybe sometime soon. Instead, she moved slowly and deliberately into his path.

"You look as if you found out something," she told him, trying not to feel too disappointed that he was wearing his detective face and regarding her with his usual calm detachment. It was, after all, what she'd really expected.

"Nothing specific," he said, frowning thoughtfully, "but I did discover that most of the men seem to like Alfred's nephew Freddie. There's a very well-stocked shop where they take care of maintenance on the farm machinery, and Freddie has a habit of borrowing tools and not returning them, but aside from that they haven't any complaints. He has an old Aston Martin he tinkers with continually. They say he's a whiz at keeping it running, and he's always ready to give a hand with the farm vehicles when he's here."

"It sounds as if there's more than one way Freddie could support himself if he wanted to," Lyndsay said. "Good mechanics are always in demand."

Quent made a wry face. "Doing something for fun isn't the same as making a living at it. A lot of people like to tinker with cars but wouldn't want to do it all day long."

"Freddie doesn't sound as bad as Alfred portrayed him, does he?" Lyndsay said. "Whitby made him sound more like a prankster than a villain. Apparently he likes to get under Alfred's skin." She went on to tell Quent what Whitby had told her. "It sounds as if the clock theft may be a nonevent. Why don't we wait until Freddie shows up and go back to being archaeologists in the meantime?" she concluded. "I'm dying to start exploring the countryside." And, she thought, despairing at the distant look on Quent's face, she was dying to get him onto another track.

"It may have been Freddie," he said, rubbing his chin thoughtfully, "but then again it may not. I've discovered that this place has its own generating system, which fails quite regularly because of overloads. That would throw the automatic timing device off until someone re-set it, which they might not do if they didn't know the power had been off."

Lyndsay frowned. "That might explain why Sofia was questioning one of the maids about whether the clock was there in the morning. But that doesn't make sense. She said she heard it later in the day. Why would she lie about it?"

"Maybe to protect Freddie, or to cover up the fact that someone discovered the timer was way off," Quent replied. "In any case, it isn't very comforting to know that Freddie can sneak in and out like a ghost. We are supposed to be protecting Marian from him, you know."

"I know," Lyndsay replied, "but from what we've heard so far he doesn't sound very threatening. I wish he'd show up so we can get a look at him for ourselves."

"So do I," Quent agreed. "Well, shall we try out some of the bicycles now? They're in an old barn just down the road a little way."

"I'm ready," Lyndsay said. She fell into step beside Quent as he retraced his path along the road, which curved away from the house toward a grove of oaks. Just beyond the trees, they came to an ancient-looking stone building. "Is this the barn?" she asked, for it looked nothing like the barns in Wisconsin.

"That's it," Quent replied. "It's one of the original farm buildings. Centuries old." He pushed open a creaky door to reveal a large, musty room and a bicycle rack, filled with bikes of assorted colors and sizes. "I'm told we can take our pick," he said. "This black one looks about right for me."

"I guess this blue one will do for me," Lyndsay said, taking hold of the handlebars and looking at it dubiously. "It looks bigger than the one I used to have. And a lot fancier."

"I think the Frobishers take their bicycle riding seriously," Quent said as he pushed his selection outside. "These are very fine quality. Well, let's give it a try. I got a general idea of the layout of the estate from one of the caretakers. It's sort of in quadrants. I thought we'd stay in the one where the house is until we're used to riding. I wouldn't want you to get too far away and not be able to make it back. Ready?"

"Ready as I'll ever be," Lyndsay replied with a sigh. Quent was back to big-brothering again. Not that her panic this morning had done anything to dispel the impression she needed it.

Quent swung onto his bike and started off. Lyndsay took a deep breath and wobbled off slowly behind him as he turned down a narrow lane with low stone walls on either side. For the first few minutes, she was too anxious about the process of riding to notice her surroundings, but soon the rhythm of riding came back to her and she was able to catch up with Quent and look around.

"There's the pond I saw from my bedroom window," she said as they rounded a bend in the road. "Oh, look! A swan! Isn't it beautiful?"

"Lovely," Quent agreed, "but a few geese might be more useful. They make good watchdogs."

"Don't you mean watchgeese?" Lyndsay asked.

"I suppose I do," Quent said, "but it doesn't sound quite right." He shook his head. "Watchgeese," he repeated, then looked over at Lyndsay and smiled. "You do have a way with words," he said.

Lyndsay smiled back, so pleased he thought she was entertaining that she forgot where she was and almost ran into him.

"Careful," Quent said, swerving to get out of her way. "Watch where you're going."

Lyndsay bit her lip and turned her attention to the road ahead. She had deserved it that time, but it was awfully hard to concentrate on riding with Quent by her side. She realized she was still distracted when he stopped suddenly and she almost panicked, jamming on her brakes and jumping off of her bike rather awkwardly. "What's wrong?" she asked, looking back at him. He was looking toward the house, a curious frown on his face.

"Did you hear something just then?" he asked. "Like a woman's scream?"

Lyndsay listened, then smiled as she realized what the sound must have been. They had passed by the pond and circled behind a walled garden. "It's Marian, singing to her flowers," she said.

Quent cocked his head, his expression a mixture of disbelief and amazement. "You're right," he said, finally smiling also. "'Red Roses for a Blue Lady.' I haven't heard that one in years. I wasn't sure whether to believe she sang to them or not. She's not bad."

"Not bad at all," Lyndsay agreed. "The high notes are a little scratchy, but she's got a lot of volume. I hope her roses appreciate it."

"I'm not sure Buff and Muff do," Quent said, laughing, as a set of canine howls joined Marian's serenade. He shook his head and pushed off on his bike again. "Marian's quite a character, isn't she?"

"A bit eccentric, but lovable," Lyndsay said. "Just the sort of person I'd imagine for the mistress of a place like this."

"And Alfred's exactly right for the master," Quent said. He looked around him, a bemused expression on his face. "It's hard to imagine places like this still exist.

When I was a boy I used to be fascinated with tales of the knights of old. King Arthur, Ivanhoe. I would have given anything to be transported back to those days."

"I read my copy of *Robin Hood* so many times that the pages were limp, and I cried at the ending every time," Lyndsay said with a sigh. "I'd have gladly deserted my family to go to Sherwood Forest. I'd still like to go back and see all of that, even though I know those times weren't anywhere near as romantic as they sounded."

"So would I," Quent agreed, "if I could be guaranteed a round-trip ticket. I wouldn't want to miss the next forty or fifty years of this age for a rerun. It's going to be a fascinating and crucial time."

There was a serious note in Quent's voice that made Lyndsay look at him quickly. "Do you mean because of the environmental problems?" she asked. She knew from some of their previous conversations that Quent was an intelligent and thoughtful man, deeply interested in the environment, and she loved to get him talking about subjects that interested her, also.

"That, and the world population. With it increasing more and more quickly. . ." At the sound of a car Quent stopped talking for a moment. "Someone's coming. You'd better get behind me. This road is very narrow."

"Yes, Quent," Lyndsay said resignedly. She dropped behind him and listened to the purr of an engine coming closer. They were below the crest of a small hill, and she couldn't see the car until it was almost upon them. It was a sports car, old but elegant, with an open top. That would have been enough in itself to rivet her attention. But it was the face of the man behind the wheel that sent her heart racing and her mind spinning dizzily. It was him! The face on the tower! No, the man on the tower had had long, silky hair. But aside from that . . .

Lyndsay was so caught up in her vision of the face that she failed to notice Quent had slowed in front of her. When he turned to look back, she suddenly realized she was about to crash into him. Immediately she jammed on her brake. Her bicycle skidded on some loose gravel and for a moment she had the sensation that everything was moving in slow motion. As the bicycle slipped sideways, she tried to put her foot down and catch herself, but her pant leg caught on the pedal and she could feel herself going down beneath the bike. She let go of the handlebars and flung her left arm up to protect her head as she hit the pavement. She was only partially successful, landing with a sharp jolt that knocked the wind out of her and gave a thump to her head that sent a hollow echo through her skull and set stars to dancing before her eyes. Stunned, she lay still, gasping for breath, her eyes scrunched closed from the pain.

"Lyndsay! Lyndsay, are you all right?" Lyndsay heard Quent's voice, strained and anxious, as if from a great distance. She felt the bicycle being lifted from on top of her. She opened her eyes just enough to see Quent drop to his knees beside her, then closed them again. His hand touched her forehead, then caressed her hair. She could feel his breath warm against her cheek. She wanted to open her eyes and see his face, but was afraid that if she did he would draw back. "Dear God," he said hoarsely, "please don't let her be badly hurt. Lyndsay, can you hear me? Lyndsay, speak to me. Are you all right? I'm afraid to move you."

Lyndsay's pains quickly receded from the forefront of her mind, replaced by a warmth that spread through her like wildfire. Quent cared about her. He really cared. She would have liked to lie there and hear more, but the genuine fear in his voice was too much for her. She opened her eyes and focused gradually on the beautiful green eyes only inches above her own. "I'm all right," she whispered. "Just help me up." She started to lift her arms to put them around his neck, but before she could do so Quent had gathered her into his arms. As he sat back on the pavement and held her close she could feel the heavy beating of his heart.

"You gave me such a scare," he whispered, his lips against her ear.

"I'm sorry," Lyndsay said, slowly turning her face toward his until their eyes met again. The intense brightness she saw in Quent's eyes nearly took her breath away. She felt as if she were seeing deep inside him, all barriers between them gone. She waited, afraid to move and break the spell. She knew that he wanted to kiss her. She could feel it in his heartbeat, read it in the shimmering lights in his irises. His eyes flicked down to her mouth and back, then rested on her mouth again. Lyndsay felt as if time stood still. Their eyes met once more. *Please kiss me,* she pleaded silently. *It's the only way I know to tell you I love you.* As if he had heard her thoughts, his body suddenly became tense, his eyes cloudy. Lyndsay was afraid he was going to back off again when suddenly, like lightning streaking from the sky and searing its way to the earth, she felt the tension rush from Quent's body and course on through hers. At the same moment his mouth took possession of hers with a mastery that left no doubt that this time he knew exactly what he was doing.

Lyndsay's mouth opened to the dizzying onslaught. She melted into Quent's strong embrace, the pain of moments before forgotten, aware only of the vibrations of emotion that coursed through her and the sensations of pleasure that made her skin come alive wherever their bodies touched. Rivers of intense longing swept between them. His arms tightened around her and he kissed his way across her cheek to her ear. Suddenly a furry body launched itself against her, and Lyndsay found her other ear being subjected to a thorough, very wet, kiss.

"Oh, don't!" Lyndsay said, pulling her head back and trying to fend off the enthusiastic dog with one hand.

"Hey, cut that out!" Quent said, as the other dog hopped and bounded beside him, trying to get his attention.

An engine sounded behind Lyndsay, then rubber squealed and the engine noise stopped. "I say, are you all right?" came a man's voice. Almost simultaneously came the sound of Marian calling, "Buff! Muff! Where are you? Oh, my goodness! What happened?" followed by running footsteps.

Lyndsay looked around and saw that same young man get out of his car and come toward them, while over Quent's shoulder she could see Marian's reddish curls bobbing. All at once she was acutely aware of the spectacle she and Quent must present, in each other's arms in the middle of the road, her fallen bike beside them on one side and Quent's bike on the other. It was a rather embarrassing situation for two supposedly serious archaeologists.

"Oh, dear," she said, and looked at Quent anxiously.

To her surprise, he seemed more dazed than upset. He surveyed the onlookers, then the little dog, which he had captured in the crook of his right arm, then stared at Lyndsay and shook his head. "Funny," he said, "but for a few minutes I could have sworn we were in Camelot."

He couldn't tell her, not yet, that in that instant when he thought she might be seriously hurt he had known beyond a shadow of a doubt that he couldn't bear the thought of life without her. He smiled at Lyndsay's up-turned face, thinking how surprised she would be to know that her accident had accomplished more in seconds than any devious plot concocted by Luke could possibly do.

CHAPTER SEVEN

"My dears, what happened?" Marian cried again, bending to peer into Quent's face. "Did you hit your head?" she asked in response to his blank stare.

Quent frowned thoughtfully. "No," he replied slowly. "I feel a little dizzy, but I think it's only a reaction to seeing Lyndsay fall. She took a nasty tumble." He put his hand carefully on Lyndsay's head. "How does your head feel?"

At the moment, Lyndsay was not sure how her head felt, she was still so electrified by Quent's kiss. Camelot? she thought dazedly. Had he said something about Camelot?

"Lyndsay, are you all right?" Marian asked, as Lyndsay studied Quent's face, wondering vaguely whether Quent was King Arthur or Sir Lancelot.

"I think she's all right," Quent finally replied for her. "She tried to stop too suddenly and her bike slipped sideways."

"That's right," Lyndsay said, returning to the present. She was about to say that Quent hadn't fallen, but quickly changed her mind. Apparently, their embrace had looked more like the result of a double disaster, and she might better leave it that way.

"Does your head hurt here?" Quent asked, his fingers having zeroed in on the lump on Lyndsay's head and extracted a wince and an "ouch" from her.

"Why do you think I said ouch?" she asked, removing his hand.

"Can you get up, dear?" Marian asked.

"Let me help," said the young man as Lyndsay nodded. "I'm Freddie Frobisher." He bent over and lifted her effortlessly to her feet. "Auntie seems to have forgotten the introductions."

"Oh, my goodness," Marian said. "I'm so sorry. Freddie, this is Dr. Lyndsay Stuart and Dr. Quentin Long. They're the archaeologists I mentioned in the message I left on your answering machine. Did you get it?"

"Of course," Freddie replied. He gave Quent a perfunctory handshake, then returned his eyes to Lyndsay, eyes that, she thought, were the most dramatically dark she had ever seen, almost as black as his hair and heavy, sweeping brows. He smiled ingratiatingly at Lyndsay. "When I looked back and saw you fall I thought perhaps it was from seeing me. I frequently have that effect on women."

"Sorry, not this time," Lyndsay said tightly. He was right, although for the wrong reason, but she wasn't about to mention that. Besides, she could feel Quent's eyes boring into her like two hot pokers, as if he thought maybe she had fallen from seeing Freddie.

"Pity," Freddie said, undaunted. "I was about to suggest you send your friend here back to the States. I'd be more than happy to show you around all the digs in this area."

"I'm afraid if anyone went it would be me," Lyndsay replied coolly. "Quent's my boss."

"Your boss, eh?" Freddie finally flicked a curious glance in Quent's direction. "I hope that's all he is."

Lyndsay could see that Quent was seething. She felt rather pleased that he was apparently jealous of the very forward Freddie, but she hoped Freddie would stop before Quent got really furious. With his black belt in karate, he could send Freddie for a spin he wouldn't soon forget. Fortunately, Marian tactfully interceded before he could bring on disaster.

"Freddie, behave yourself," she said mildly. To Lyndsay she said, "Don't mind him. He thinks he's got to capture the heart of every female he meets." Then she redirected her attention to Freddie. "What kind of mischief have you been into since I've been away?"

"Been working my head off, actually," Freddie replied. "I was up most of last night wiring up a sound system for a big-wheel rock star. When I got in and got your message I decided to come straight up for a few days of R and R." He smiled suggestively at Lyndsay again. "And am I ever glad that I did. Can I give you a lift back to the house?"

"No, thanks, I'll walk." Lyndsay said quickly. "I feel fine."

"How about you, Auntie?" Freddie asked next.

"Not if you still won't let Buff and Muff in your silly car," Marian replied, making a disgusted face at Freddie.

Freddie gave an exaggerated shrug and then cocked an eyebrow at Quent. "So be it. I don't suppose you'd like a lift?"

"As a matter of fact, I would," Quent replied smoothly, now back in control of himself. "I've been looking forward to meeting you. One of the men, Smithers I believe it was, was telling me about your car earlier. If Marian wouldn't mind walking my bicycle back for me..." He looked inquiringly at Marian, who smiled delightedly.

"Of course not. Do go on and get acquainted with Freddie. Freddie, dear, tell Sofia to set another place for luncheon. We'll be ready in about an hour."

Lyndsay watched as Quent got into the passenger side of Freddie's car. He was a half a head taller than Freddie, and much more muscular, although Freddie looked as if he worked out some himself. But, she thought with an inward sigh, it was no doubt which one was the real man. Too bad Freddie thought he had to try so hard. He really was quite handsome, although his face was a little narrow. Now that she'd seen him up close, it didn't seem quite so much like the face she'd seen on the tower, after all. That face had been broader, less angular. But then, it could have been the angle of view.

As the Aston Martin went on toward the house, Lyndsay walked along beside Marian, pushing her bike, feeling a dull thump in her head with every step. Marian chattered on about her flowers, the dogs trotted beside them, and Lyndsay silently wondered what Quent had in mind, going off with Freddie. Did he plan to size him up generally, or ask some specific questions? She could tell from the way he had jumped at Freddie's invitation that his mind was back in detective mode again. Everything had happened so fast that she could scarcely believe he had kissed her so passionately. The way everyone else had misinterpreted what had happened, it almost seemed as if the bump on her head had knocked her silly and she had imagined it. If Quent hadn't said what he had about Camelot—

"Here we are." Marian interrupted her musings by taking her arm and leading her toward a garden gate. "Come in here and sit down for a few minutes. I'm sure those two men will be talking cars for a while, anyway. Would you like something cool to drink?''

"Yes, thank you," Lyndsay said, then stopped and caught her breath as a burst of scent filled her nostrils and a dazzling array of color filled her eyes. "Ooh," she exclaimed, "how lovely! This looks and smells like heaven." Marian had taken her into the rose garden Lyndsay had seen from her window. From above, it had looked merely like concentric circles of blossoming bushes separated by brick pathways, surrounding a small reflecting pool beside which set a low wooden bench. But on the ground, the beauty was almost overwhelming.

"My pride and joy," Marian said, beaming. "All my prize roses are here. This garden has been featured in several gardening magazines."

"I can certainly understand why," Lyndsay said.

"Well, you just sit down and enjoy it while I see about getting us a drink."

Marian hurried off and Lyndsay sat down on the bench, her eyes roaming slowly around the circle of flowers. The deep green of the lush ivy on the low garden walls was a perfect foil for the brilliant colors of the roses, which Marian had planted so that each circle had a full range of colors, from white to deepest red. As a backdrop, the shape of Gravelpick Manor seemed less foreboding, for on the rear of the building the ancient gray stones were heavily covered with ivy. As she looked, she saw Tessie lean out of one of the second-story windows and give her feather duster a shake. With her quaint triangular white cap and dark dress she looked like a maiden of long ago, leaning out to call to her suitor far below. Lyndsay could imagine Quent in a velvet cape, throwing caution to the winds and climbing the ivy vines to her own boudoir. How romantic that would be. If the vines didn't give way.

The sight of Buff and Muff rollicking her way brought Lyndsay back to reality. Quent was not likely to try anything so foolish. In fact, he had probably already forgotten he had kissed her again, or at least managed to excuse it as a momentary lapse brought on by seeing her fall. "Camelot? I don't remember anything about Camelot," she could imagine him saying. She sighed and bent to pat Buff and Muff. "Too bad I can't ask you two to testify," she said dryly. "You heard him say that, didn't you?"

"I am sorry we took so long," Marian said as she drew near, "but I went looking for my ice pack to put on your bump. Alfie never puts things back where they should be. Here, see if this won't make it feel better." She handed Lyndsay a waterproof bag filled with ice and then sat down beside her just as Whitby drifted noiselessly toward them, bearing a silver tray with two tall glasses.

"Thank you," Lyndsay said, smiling at both of them. She put the ice pack on her head, then took a sip of the rose-colored liquid in the glass. "Mmm. This is delicious. What is it?"

"Raspberry tea on shaved ice," Marian replied. "I don't know if it has any medicinal properties, but it always perks me up." She took a long drink of her tea, then set it on the seat beside her and leaned toward Lyndsay. "I think it's terribly fortunate that Freddie came up for a visit, don't you?" she said in confidential tones. "The way he flirts, he's already made your Quent jealous. That's the best way I know to get a man to move off the mark. I had to use it on my Alfie. Funny how men who are strong and brave otherwise can be so afraid to let their real feelings out, isn't it?"

Lyndsay stared at her. "Well, uh, I'm not sure he has real feelings . . ." she croaked, amazed at Marian's presumption. She'd always heard the British were more reticent than Americans!

"Of course he does," Marian said with a positive nod. "I've been watching him, and it's as plain as day. I've been watching you, too, and I can see that you're tired of waiting for him to make a move. But don't worry. Gravelpick Manor may not look it, but it's a perfect place for romance to blossom."

Alfred Frobisher had certainly been right on the mark when he called his wife a matchmaker, Lyndsay thought as she took another sip of her tea. She smiled at the little woman. "I guess I'm glad to hear that," she said, "but I'm not so sure Quent would be. Every time I think he's getting interested, he backs off again."

Marian nodded. "Just like Alfie. But don't worry, he'll come around. It's obvious that you two were made for each other. Why, you even share the same profession. That's a real bonus."

"Yes, I suppose it is," Lyndsay agreed, although it wasn't the profession Marian thought it was.

"Shall we go in for lunch?" Marian said as she finished her tea. "I'm famished. And I'm rather curious about how those two men are getting on, aren't you?"

"Yes, I am," Lyndsay agreed. She not only wanted to see if Quent would still act jealous, but she also wanted to see if she could tell from his expression whether he had learned anything about Freddie's possible involvement with the missing clock.

The two men were already in the breakfast room when Lyndsay and Marian entered. They stood up courteously, Quent looking his usual calm self, giving no clue about what he and Freddie might have been discussing, but Freddie smiling broadly.

"There's the lovely Lyndsay again," he said. "Even lovelier than Auntie's roses."

Lyndsay thought she saw a brief flicker of anger in Quent's eyes. Perhaps it wouldn't hurt to fan the flames a little, she thought. She smiled sweetly at Freddie. "Now, Freddie," she said, "keep that up and you just might turn my head."

"Then I'll definitely keep it up," Freddie replied.

That remark brought a real spark to Quent's eyes, but Lyndsay doubted anyone else had noticed it as he glanced toward the ice pack she'd set on the table beside her and asked solicitously, "Is your head still hurting?"

"It's feeling better," she replied. "Just a little achy now."

"Did you remember to bring some aspirin with you?" he asked. "If you didn't, I have some in my room."

"Oh, I have some," Lyndsay said. "If I still need it, I'll get it after lunch."

"You probably ought to lie down for a little while," Quent said.

"I may do that." Lyndsay could see out of the corner of her eye that Freddie was following this little exchange with amusement. Now he laughed outright.

"Does Quent always hover over you like that?" he asked. "He sounds as if he thinks you need a keeper."

Quent gave Freddie a look that could have melted steel, but before he could say anything Marian interceded. "Quent is being thoughtful, Freddie. You ought to try it sometime. By the way, Quent, what did you think of Freddie's car? He seems to think it's the most magnificent thing in the world, but as far as I'm concerned it's just a machine."

Quent smiled, his calm regained. "It's a magnificent machine," he said. "I think I might be tempted to work on one of that vintage, without all the pollution control devices we have on the new ones. They're impossible to figure out."

"But so necessary," Marian said. "When I was in Bavaria last summer and saw what's happening to the Black Forest from the acid rain I was just sick. Absolutely sick."

Lyndsay soon gathered that Marian was a devoted environmentalist. Since Quent was very knowledgeable on the subject, they got into quite a discussion, but Freddie seemed bored, spending most of his time gazing speculatively at Lyndsay from beneath his thick black lashes. Alfred was right about one thing, she thought. Freddie was a very self-centered young man, whose main concern was his own pleasure.

When the luncheon drew to a close, Freddie glanced at Lyndsay and then at Quent. "If you'd still like to take a spin in the Aston Martin, you're welcome to take it out yourself," he said. "I think I'd just as soon hang around the house."

"I'm afraid I'm not up to handling it and trying to learn to drive on the left at the same time," Quent said mildly, although his eyes had followed Freddie's and his expression was what Lyndsay would have described as lethally calm.

Marian, whom Lyndsay could see missed very little, quickly spoke up. "Freddie, if you promised Quent a spin in the countryside, go and do it. Right now. Shoo. I'll take care of Lyndsay."

"Yes, Auntie," Freddie said resignedly. He gave Lyndsay a broad wink. "Get rested up. We'll have some fun later."

When the men had gone, Marian shook her head. "I'm afraid Freddie is a little heavy-handed. Quent doesn't need that much prodding. He's apt to thrash him, and we don't want that. I do think things are going rather well, though. We'll have a little dinner party this evening, just the four of us. We can even dance in the foyer. That should be fun. Next weekend we'll have a real party. Now, would you like to lie down in your room for a while? I always take a little siesta myself."

"Yes, I think I'd like that," Lyndsay said, for her head was aching more now. She wasn't sure whether it was from the fall or from the tension she had felt growing between Quent and Freddie all during lunch. Marian might have been right that jealousy was good for Quent, but it made her very uncomfortable. She would hate Quent to think she was really interested in Freddie.

As she and Marian walked down the long hallway toward the foyer, Marian pointed out several more of the ancestral paintings on the walls. "That rascal got himself killed fighting with Napoleon at the battle of Waterloo," she said, indicating a florid gentleman with a handlebar mustache. "The old fool volunteered when he was past sixty." A few steps farther on she stopped in front of the picture of Frederick again. "Remarkable how much our Freddie looks like him, isn't it?" she said. "Not to mention having the same kind of interest in the opposite sex."

"Incredible," Lyndsay agreed. "That's why I fell off my bicycle. When he drove by, just for a second I thought I was seeing a ghost."

"Goodness, I should have warned you, shouldn't I?" Marian said. "I didn't think a scientist who digs around in old tombs and such would believe in ghosts."

"Oh, I don't," Lyndsay replied quickly. "I was just startled by the similarity."

At the top of the stairs, Marian went in the opposite direction toward her room and Lyndsay moved slowly past the eight doors, wishing Marian had not brought up the subject of the ghost again. Since Freddie had just come from London, his couldn't possibly have been the face she'd seen on the tower. Could she have imagined it after seeing that picture? She hated to think she was that suggestible.

Once in her room, Lyndsay quickly went into the bath and found her aspirin. The bathroom, she was happy to find, had been done over fairly recently, and it was light and modern. She decided to put off bathing until closer to dinnertime, went back into the bedroom, turned back the coverlet and prepared to lie down. Suddenly it seemed as if the whole room were suffused in a golden light and the scent of roses from below was almost as strong as it had been in the garden. Perhaps, she thought, a storm was brewing, doing tricks with the light and the air. She went to the window and looked out. No, there were still only a few fleecy clouds in the sky. As if drawn by a magnet, her gaze moved upward to the tower. Her heart stopped, and an icy chill ran through her. The man was there in one of the notches again, looking straight at her, that wistful smile on his face.

For a moment, Lyndsay couldn't move. Then her heart started racing and she jumped away from the window and bolted for the door. She couldn't stay in this room! Not for another minute! She flew down the hallway, down the stairs and, without knowing why, ran into the library and flung herself down in one of the chairs beside the fireplace, still trembling. Dear Lord, she thought, she was losing her mind! She was having hallucinations. Ghosts weren't real. Every sane person knew that!

"Just take it easy," she told herself, trying to slow her pounding heartbeat. "You didn't sleep much last night. You've got a vivid imagination. Breathe deeply and close your eyes. Think about Quent. Think about his golden hair and beautiful green eyes. He's real. Think about him. Imagine you're kissing him. His arms are around you..." It took several minutes for Lyndsay's self-prescribed therapy to work, but at last she stopped trembling and began to feel warm and drowsy. She put her feet up on the hassock in front of the chair and leaned her head back. A few minutes later, she was asleep.

She slept so soundly that it seemed at first the voice she heard saying her name was part of a dream, but at last she opened her eyes to find Quent bending over her, a worried frown crinkling his forehead.

"What are you doing down here?" he asked. "I had a devil of a time finding you. I thought you'd be in your room."

"Oh!" Lyndsay straightened to a sitting position, as the memory of her flight came back to her in a rush. "I—I wasn't comfortable lying down," she invented quickly. "It made my head hurt. I remembered seeing these chairs, so I came down here to nap."

"Damn! I should have checked you over more carefully," Quent said, looking even more anxious as he bent farther and scrutinized Lyndsay's eyes closely. "How does your head feel now? We don't want you going around with a concussion that should be tended to."

"Much better, thanks," Lyndsay said, feeling a sudden rush of warmth at Quent's concern. He was so sweet. She was foolish to resent the way he tried to take care of her. It showed he really did care. "Do my eyes look all right?'' she asked as Quent kept looking first at one, then the other.

"What? Oh, yes, fine," he said, straightening quickly to his full height. "Better than fine," he added with a strangely bemused little smile.

"That's good," Lyndsay said, wondering what that smile might mean. She glanced at her watch. "Goodness, it's almost four o'clock. Did you just get back from your drive?"

"About a half hour ago," Quent replied. "Freddie insisted on driving to North Twickham to see some people, then around past an old ruined abbey not far from here. It's an interesting place. You'll have to see it."

"I'd like to," Lyndsay said. "Did you find out anything useful?"

Quent glanced around the room. "Let's take a little walk outside," he said, holding out his hand to help Lyndsay up from her chair.

Lyndsay took his hand without thinking. Then, as his warm, strong fingers closed around hers, she felt a surge of happiness that almost took her breath away. She loved the way his hold made her feel, so safe and secure. She loved Quent, just the way he was. She wouldn't change a thing.

"Head still feel okay?" he asked as she stood and stared at him, smiling a little dazedly at her new understanding.

"Absolutely," she said, feeling her bump with her free hand. "A little sore to the touch, that's all."

"It's a good thing you have such thick hair," Quent said, "but I think if we're going to ride very far you should get one of those little helmets cyclists wear."

Lyndsay smiled. "I will if you will."

Quent raised his eyebrows, then smiled back. "Fair enough." He started to let go of Lyndsay's hand, but when she clung to his he looked down at her and smiled again, tightening his own grip as he led her out the door.

"Mind telling me why you didn't want to talk inside?" Lyndsay asked when they were on the road, walking side by side along the road toward the main gate.

"Just being cautious," Quent replied. "I wouldn't put it past Freddie to have the place bugged."

"Really?" Lyndsay stopped and stared at Quent. "Then you think he's capable of doing something as awful as Alfred thought?"

"I doubt it," Quent said, shaking his head, "but I'm not sure what to make of him yet. He seems friendly and open. Everywhere we went, people waved to him. He stopped to talk to some men at a hardware store, and it was plain they like him. He's obviously not a snob. But I also got the impression there's a lot more underneath than Alfred gives him credit for. He's well-informed about world affairs. Seems rather passionately interested in the troubles in Northern Ireland."

"That doesn't explain why you think he might have bugged the library," Lyndsay said as Quent paused, frowning.

Quent shrugged. "I got the feeling that he could be very cold and calculating if necessary, not that he'd have to be to bug the house. He mentioned bugging a room for a friend once. That doesn't necessarily mean he's up to anything evil, though. He might do it just to entertain himself, or someone else."

"Someone else? Who?"

"Anyone who wanted to know what was going on when they weren't here," Quent replied, giving Lyndsay what she thought was a rather strangely analytical look.

"Do you mean like Alfred wanting to keep track of Marian, or of them wanting to know what the servants are up to?" she asked.

"Possibly." He cleared his throat and assumed a more stoic expression. "What do you think of Freddie?"

Lyndsay debated saying she thought he was terribly handsome and charming but decided against it. It would only make Quent unhappy. Instead, she said, "I'm not sure I like him. I don't like men who come on so strong."

Quent smiled wryly. "I don't like that aspect of his personality, either, but he's awfully good at it. He was flirting with all of the girls we saw in North Twickham, and they were batting their eyelashes at him like Marian at her best."

Lyndsay sighed. "So far, we have an intelligent, flirtatious, likable rascal who likes to play pranks. Not very scary, but that does make him a prime candidate for the clock thief, doesn't it? Do you think he took it?"

"I haven't the slightest idea from anything he said," Quent replied, "but I wouldn't be at all surprised if it turned up suddenly and mysteriously while he's here. And, if it does—" he paused and gave Lyndsay a serious, meaningful look "—I'm going to take it apart, very carefully."

"You are? Why?" Lyndsay asked, then when Quent frowned reprovingly, she realized he wanted her to think like a detective. What was it she was missing? It came to her in a flash. "A bomb?" she squeaked.

"It's a possibility," he said. "One we can't afford to overlook. That clock sits right above the spot where Marian apparently sits in the evening."

"And Alfred, too," Lyndsay said. "Oh, my. What a horrible idea. I can't imagine Freddie doing something like that. He'd have to be crazy."

"Or, as Alfred mentioned, in desperate need of money. He has the life-style of a millionaire, but he had to hit me up for the price of a tank of petrol, as they call it, while we were out." Quent sighed heavily. "Let's sit down for a while. I'm tired." He walked over to a grassy bank beside the road and sat down cross-legged, leaning his chin on his hand, staring pensively into the distance.

"What's wrong, Quent?" Lyndsay asked as she sat down beside him, for he looked deeply troubled.

Quent looked at her and smiled crookedly. "It's just that I'd hate to find out that things here aren't really what they seem to be, so beautiful and old and peaceful. It's almost like a dream. And Freddie. Strange as it seems, I admire him. He's everything I could never be." He paused. "Maybe envy is a better word."

"Envy?" Lyndsay studied Quent curiously. She couldn't imagine him envying anyone, let alone Freddie. "You mean, because of all this?" she asked with a sweeping gesture encompassing the Gravelpick land.

"Only in the sense that he takes it all so much for granted," Quent replied. "He has roots here that go back for centuries, while I . . . I don't even know where my great-grandfather came from."

"I suppose that does give him a sense of security," Lyndsay said thoughtfully. "He acts as if he doesn't have a care in the world."

"Exactly," Quent said. He plucked a blade of grass and chewed on it, staring meditatively into the distance as he spoke. "Freddie seems suspended at a stage in life I missed completely. Fast cars, pretty girls, exciting parties, lots of friends. When my father left us, I got old right away. I became obsessed with the idea of finding out where he had gone and why, how he could have left the family who thought he loved them. I never did find out all the answers, but I did learn almost everything there is to know about how to track someone down. So I became a detective, and that's all I'll ever be.''

Lyndsay felt tears prick at her eyes. How sad, she thought, that Quent still felt so bitter. Some hurts could never be erased. But he shouldn't think he was less a man than Freddie. In her book, he was twice the man or more. She put her hand on his arm. "Try not to think about yesterday," she said softly. "I like you just the way you are today. You're the finest man I've ever known."

Quent stared at her. Did she really mean that? he wondered. It seemed she did. Her eyes were so misty and soft and beautiful. He wanted to hold her and make her feel happy and loved, but instead put his hand over hers, caressing her delicate skin with his forefinger. "Are you sure?" he asked. "Don't you wish I'd quit nagging at you about stupid things? I know you think I'm patronizing, that I don't think you can take care of yourself. But I don't mean it the way it sounds. I—I do it because . . ."

He stopped, choking back the lump in his throat. There was so much he wanted to tell her, but this was not the time. It had only been this morning that he'd discovered the depth of his own feelings. He needed to think carefully about just what to tell her and how to find out how sure she was of her own feelings. Meanwhile, he could tell her something that must be pretty obvious, anyway, every time he looked at her. He laid his hand against the velvety softness of her cheek and smiled gently. "I do it because I care so much about you," he said.

CHAPTER EIGHT

HEARING QUENT say those words brought real tears to Lyndsay's eyes. That was far more than she'd hoped to hear him say, even though she already knew it was the truth. Perhaps being jealous of Freddie was a good thing, after all. She smiled through her tears. "I know," she said. "I don't really mind—in fact I like it. As long as you don't overdo it."

"Like yesterday?" Quent asked with a rueful smile.

"Yes, like yesterday. What on earth was wrong with you?" She didn't really expect any further confessions, but it was worth a try.

"Oh, just uptight about several things, I guess," Quent replied, confirming Lyndsay's negative expectations. He glanced at his watch. "I expect we'd better be getting back to the house. Marian said they were going to skip tea today and have dinner at seven in honor of our American stomachs."

"That's very thoughtful of her," Lyndsay said, grasping Quent's offered hand tightly as he got up and pulled her to her feet. "I'm afraid my stomach doesn't have any idea what time it is, though. It seems like today is just a continuation of yesterday."

"I suppose in a way it does," Quent said, "but then again in some ways it seems like yesterday was a hundred years ago."

His voice had such an intense note that Lyndsay first glanced and then stared at him. He was studying her so intently that she imagined she could see the shadows of his thoughts deep in his eyes. At first they were dark, then gradually flickering shafts of light seemed to emerge, charging the air around them with a current that made Lyndsay's heart beat faster. It was almost as if they were communicating at some mystical, elemental level, as if she could feel what Quent was feeling without him saying a word. When his eyes moved down to rest on her lips, she could feel her lips begin to tingle. She held very still, breathlessly watching the thick fringe of his lashes and the soft curve of his mouth. *Kiss me, Quent,* her mind said over and over. Please, kiss me. Don't be afraid. But he made no move toward her. Instead, the tiny lines around his eyes slowly deepened, his lips curved into a smile, and he looked into her eyes once again.

"What were you thinking?" Lyndsay asked, not wanting the moment to end.

"Many things." Quent's smile widened and he chuckled softly. "One of them was what it might be like if we could go back in time to centuries ago, like we were talking about earlier. I was wondering what a man in one of those suits of armor did when he wanted to hug a woman. Did he ask her to wait a few minutes while he took it off?"

Lyndsay wrinkled her nose at him. That unromantic reply had certainly shattered the spell. "She probably carried a can opener," she replied.

Quent threw back his head and roared with laughter. "I can picture you, working away and muttering to yourself the way you do sometimes, while I stand there sweating and hoping you won't slip and cut me instead of

the armor," he explained when his laughter had sub-
sided.

"You have a ridiculous imagination," Lyndsay said,
smiling up at him as they started walking back toward the
house. "Maybe you should be a comedian. That story
you came up with about Mora Mora was a riot. It was all
I could do to keep a straight face."

"That was pretty inspired, wasn't it?" he said with a
grin. "I used to make up stuff like that when I was a kid.
I had imaginary adventures in all kinds of strange places
and times. I spent most of one summer in a big oak tree
in our backyard, pretending I was Tarzan of the jun-
gle."

"Really? I spent a summer up a tree, too, being Rob-
inson Crusoe," Lyndsay said. "I fixed a place to sleep
and everything. It was great until I fell out and broke my
arm."

They continued to reminisce lightheartedly about their
childhoods as they walked along. Maybe, Lyndsay
thought hopefully, Quent's remembering the happy times
in his life before his father had gone away was a good
sign. He needed something to give him a new perspec-
tive on his early years.

Whitby greeted them at the door with his usual pleas-
antly deferential air. "Madam said to tell you," he said,
"that you should dress for dinner this evening, and to
come to the library for cocktails as soon as you're ready."

"Dress?" Quent said, raising his eyebrows. "Does that
mean formal dress?"

"Yes, sir," Whitby replied.

Quent shook his head. "Whitby, I'm afraid, like most
American college professors, I don't own formal attire.
I rent it on those rare occasions it's required. What shall

I do? For that matter, what will Dr. Stuart do? I doubt she's brought anything suitable, either.''

''Yes, I have,'' Lyndsay said quickly. ''I anticipated it might be necessary.''

''Oh,'' Quent said with a frown, and Lyndsay almost laughed aloud. He must have thought she really had followed his packing instructions to the letter.

''I believe a dark suit will be all right, if you have one of those, sir,'' Whitby said, looking a little perplexed.

''Yes, I do have,'' Quent said. A few moments later as he and Lyndsay climbed the staircase together he remarked in an undertone, ''I think I just confirmed Whitby's view that we colonials are still savages.''

''Only the males,'' Lyndsay said, and laughed as Quent gave her a dark look. ''I knew the British often dress for dinner. They do it in all of the books. I'll see you later, in one of my best gowns.'' She gave Quent an airy wave and went on into her room. To her surprise, one of the younger maids was already there, waiting for her.

''My name's Maura. Madam sent me to help you get ready for dinner,'' the girl said. ''Would you like me to draw your bath now?''

''Why, yes, thanks. Go ahead,'' Lyndsay replied. Apparently, she thought wryly, Sofia had reported to Marian her opinion that the savage colonials didn't know how to behave when offered the usual services of a fine home, and so Marian had taken matters into her own hands. Well, it was all right with her. Not only would it be fun to live like the beautiful people for a while, but seeing the open window with the curtains still blowing in the wind had forcibly reminded her of her two ghostly encounters. She was very glad to have someone in the bedroom with her. She doubted ghosts liked crowds.

After her bath, Lyndsay discovered that Maura had already laid out her jade-green silk. "I think this should be just right for tonight," she said, making Lyndsay wonder if Marian had given the girl some kind of instructions about that, too, for the dress was as close to sexy as anything she owned. The crisscrossed bodice showed her curves to advantage but was not really daringly revealing. Maura also helped Lyndsay do her hair, wielding a curling wand so skilfully that Lyndsay asked if she'd had training.

"No, ma'am," Maura replied with a grin, "but I've got five sisters. We do each other's hair all the time."

By the time Lyndsay was ready, she felt more glamorous than she could ever remember feeling. *If that doesn't put Quent in a romantic mood, nothing will,* she thought as she surveyed the results in a mirror. It would probably elicit some comments from Freddie, too, though hopefully nothing that would make Quent really upset. Now that things were progressing so well between them, she did not want another setback. She went into the hall and walked to the head of the stairs. Below, in the foyer, she could hear voices. Matchmaking Marian had apparently delayed everyone there so that Quent would witness her grand entrance, she thought, suddenly feeling nervous. She took a deep breath and started slowly down the stairs. About halfway down, she caught sight of the three of them. Marian had positioned herself so she could watch the stairs, and as soon as she saw Lyndsay, she smiled.

"There she is now," she said.

Both Quent and Freddie turned to look upward, but Quent's face was all Lyndsay saw. She was sure that no matter how many exciting and fascinating things happened to her for the rest of her life, she would never forget his expression the moment he saw her. Totally dumbstruck, he let his jaw quite literally drop. Only his eyes seemed to have escaped the general paralysis of movement that had taken over his face. They were so bright and alive that Lyndsay could almost feel their glow across the space between them. She tried to concentrate carefully on taking each step downward, for her pulse was racing erratically. Quent's reaction to her appearance was exciting enough, without her own reaction to his. He was wearing a dark blue suit she'd never seen before, and he looked so unbearably handsome that just looking at him made her head swim.

"Wow," Freddie said, whistling softly. "That is one gorgeous lady."

"Thank you, Freddie," Lyndsay said, at last looking at him. Freddie was wearing an elegant tuxedo, obviously custom-tailored to his slender frame. "You're looking very handsome tonight yourself." She looked back at Quent. "And so are you."

Quent smiled a little dazedly. "I don't know who would notice either Freddie or me if you were in the room. You're the most beautiful creature I've ever seen."

"Why, Quent, what a lovely thing to say." Lyndsay blinked back the tears of happiness that had sprung to her eyes.

Freddie's gaze darted back and forth between them for a moment as if he was trying to figure something out, then he grinned wickedly. "I say, Quent old fellow, I don't believe you've been giving this fair lady the proper ration of compliments. You'd better get off the mark or you're going to get left behind. Choice morsels like Lyndsay don't go to the slow and indecisive." He made a gallant, sweeping bow and then held out his arm to Lyndsay. "May I escort you into the library? I believe

Aunt Marian has brought out some of her best champagne.''

''Thank you,'' Lyndsay said, smiling as warmly as she could manage at him as she took his arm. She really wanted to be on Quent's arm, but she couldn't avoid Freddie without appearing rude. She hoped Quent wouldn't get the idea that she was happy with the situation and start looking daggers at Freddie the way he had at lunch.

Quent, however, did not seem especially annoyed at the attention Freddie was giving Lyndsay. His face seemed frozen in a sort of half-smiling mask. Only his eyes, when they met hers, gave away the fact that something was going on inside his head. They were still intense, but now more speculative than adoring. Lyndsay could not for the life of her figure out what that look meant. Was he trying to figure out something about her or Freddie or both? She would have liked to ask him, but Freddie continued to hover near her as they drank their champagne and monopolized the conversation with a series of hilarious stories about his life in London. He was such an excellent raconteur that Lyndsay couldn't help laughing at his jokes. She noticed that Quent's laughter was rather subdued but decided if he was determined to spend the evening brooding about something, then that was his problem. She was doing no more than any well-bred guest would do.

After a short time, Whitby announced that dinner was served, and this time Marian almost forcibly took Freddie's arm, giving Lyndsay an encouraging smile as she did so.

As Lyndsay took Quent's arm, she smiled up at him. ''I think I know how Cinderella felt,'' she said.

"You should. I think you've charmed the prince," Quent said in a rather sour undertone.

Lyndsay couldn't believe her ears. Did Quent actually think she'd been flirting with Freddie? She scowled at him, but the look missed its mark. He stared straight ahead as Marian led them through the huge dining room Lyndsay had seen earlier into a smaller one with a table elegantly set for four.

"This is the family dining room," she said as she took her seat. "That monstrosity we came through is called the state dining room. I believe two or three presidents of the United States have dined there when they had business with the family. Some of the Frobishers used to be in the arms business."

"Auntie," Freddie said reprovingly, "they still are. The Frobisher Munitions Company is one of the leading suppliers of automatic weapons."

Marian gave him a disgusted look. "I know, but I don't approve of it. There's nothing I can do about it, though, so I try to ignore it."

Freddie grinned at Quent and shook his head. "Women do have very strange minds, don't they?" he said.

"I'm afraid I'm not as expert on the subject as you are," Quent replied coolly. "Lyndsay's mind seems to work quite well...most of the time." He cocked a meaningful eyebrow at Lyndsay.

"Why, thank you, Dr. Long," she said, flashing a brilliant if insincere smile in his direction. She hoped he got the message that she was not going to turn into a dull little mouse just to pacify him. If he wanted to stake his claim to her, he would have to break out of his shell and do it positively, not negatively.

"Ah, yes, a doctor of archaeology," Freddie said. He smiled sedutively at Lyndsay. "Auntie told me you dug up some frozen chap in Siberia. I'm surprised that smile of yours didn't thaw him out immediately."

Lyndsay sighed. "You do know how to turn everything into flattery, don't you? Of course, it's true, he did thaw out so fast that we were afraid he'd spoil, but I just pretended I was angry with him and gave him a look that froze him right up again."

The general laughter greeting that remark made Lyndsay feel quite pleased with herself. Even Quent had laughed. And that time she had meant to be funny.

The dinner conversation continued to be light and witty, but Lyndsay noticed that Quent now seemed to be avoiding looking at her, and he had very little to say. She began to have second thoughts about jealousy as a way to further their relationship. She could tell Marian had noticed his silence, too, when she asked Quent to tell more about Mora Mora. To Lyndsay's relief, he obliged with some outlandish tales of Mora Moran fertility rites, which, she thought, at least indicated his mind wasn't completely obsessed with some ridiculous worries about her and Freddie. Finally he brought the subject around to the religious ceremonies of the fictitious people, which then led to the topic of the old abbey Freddie had shown him.

"You must take Lyndsay to see the place," Marian said, her eyes sparkling with matchmaking zeal. "It's only about two miles from here. Just a nice little bike ride. If it's a fine day tomorrow, I'll have Cook pack you a picnic lunch to take along."

"That sounds like a good idea," Quent agreed. "I'd planned to take her there myself." He gave Lyndsay a rather defiant glance, which made her wonder if he actually had the ridiculous notion she might refuse.

"That sounds like a wonderful idea to me, too," Lyndsay said, hoping to alleviate his suspicions. "I'd like to see that strange ruin you have here, too. Alfred made it sound quite interesting. He said it might have been a family burial tomb."

"You don't want to see that old wreck," Freddie said with a grimace. "It's nothing but a filthy hovel. It might fall in on you if you aren't careful."

"But Freddie, that's just the kind of place that archaeologists love," Lyndsay said. "The dirtier, the better. That means no one's disturbed it, unless, of course, the dirt consists of beer cans and such."

"I'd still strongly recommend you stay away from that ruin, unless you want another bump on your pretty head," Freddie said.

"I'll see that she does," Quent said, giving Lyndsay a look so commanding that she decided to drop the subject. Apparently he took Freddie's admonitions as a sign the place was really dangerous.

Freddie glanced at his watch and stood up. "Aunt Marian, if you'll excuse me I need to make a phone call, and then I can set up some tapes for dancing in the foyer, if you still want to do that."

"Oh, yes," Marian said. "I think it's good to move around a bit after a big meal. Nothing too fast, though. I think we're all getting tired. It's been a long, busy day." She made a face at Freddie's departing back. "I can't stand that rock and roll music Freddie's so crazy about. People look like they're having seizures when they try to dance to it. I had Freddie make some tapes with nice old-fashioned melodies and good rhythms."

Lyndsay wondered what Marian meant by old-fashioned, but a few minutes later she heard in the distance the sound of one of the hits from the big-band era. "That's nice for dancing," she said as Marian stood up and invited Quent to take both of them "to the dance." She had no idea whether Quent liked to dance, but she hoped he wasn't going to let Freddie take over again. If he didn't want her paying attention to Freddie, it was time for him to assert himself. Besides, she wanted to be in Quent's arms, not Freddie's. However, as soon as they reached the foyer, Freddie made a sweeping bow before her and then whisked her away before she could say a word.

"Aunt Marian taught me. She used to be a professional, you know," he said when Lyndsay commented on his skill. "Maybe she can teach your friend a few new steps. He looks a bit stiff."

"He also looks as if he'd like to kill me," Lyndsay said, catching an icy glare from Quent, who was dancing with Marian, over Freddie's shoulder. "Don't hold me so tight."

Freddie chuckled and swirled off into the darker space beneath the staircase. "Maybe we should try a little slower dancing," he said, releasing Lyndsay's hand and putting both arms around her.

"Stop that, Freddie," Lyndsay said, as his hands became a little too familiar and he nuzzled her ear with his lips.

"You wanted to make that boss of yours jealous, didn't you?" Freddie said, pulling his head back and grinning as Lyndsay scowled at him. "Don't worry, I know the score. It won't hurt him to fume and seethe a bit more. Any man who could work with you day after day and not go out of his mind from wanting you is pretty slow. I'd have propositioned you the first day.''

''Not all men are like that,'' Lyndsay said stiffly.

Freddie raised a skeptical eyebrow. ''No, some of them lie about it,'' he said. He tightened his hold on Lyndsay and rubbed his cheek against hers. ''Are you sure old Quent is the man for you?''

''Very sure,'' Lyndsay replied. ''Now let's...''

She had no time to finish suggesting they go back out where Quent and Marian were, for the pair suddenly appeared beside them.

''Having fun back here?'' Quent asked in a voice that could have sawed a log in half.

One quick look at Quent's glaring eyes, and Freddie released Lyndsay and stepped back. ''No, old chap. Actually, I've struck out,'' he said with an ingratiating smile. ''Shall we change partners?''

''Let's,'' Quent agreed. He waited until Freddie had moved away with Marian and then turned his scowl on Lyndsay. ''Haven't you any sense at all?'' he demanded in an undertone.

''That,'' Lyndsay replied, ''is a stupid question.'' She held up her arms. ''We'd better dance. We're guests here, in case you'd forgotten.''

''No, I hadn't forgotten,'' Quent growled as he clamped her into a viselike grip and began moving in time to the music, ''but I didn't think it meant going overboard to please your hosts.''

''I did not go overboard,'' Lyndsay snapped. ''You're imagining things.''

''Oh, really?'' Quent's mouth was downturned, his eyes icy. ''You giggled like a silly teenager at everything Freddie said, then let him take you here behind the stairs and paw you. Don't tell me I'm imagining things.''

"Oh, yes, you are," Lyndsay retorted. "I laughed when he was funny and I told him to quit it when he tried to paw me. Not that it's any of your business. I'm your employee, and so far as I know, that's all that I am. If you're jealous, I'd like to know why."

"I am not jealous," Quent denied, his eyes flashing. "I did think we were friends. I think that gives me some right to tell you when your behavior is out of line. Perhaps you'd prefer it if I didn't give a damn when you made a fool of yourself."

"You're the one who's making a fool of himself," Lyndsay snapped. "You're so jealous your face is almost as green as your eyes."

"Don't be ridiculous," Quent said, giving Lyndsay a disgusted look. "Jealousy is childish. Besides, I...I have no reason to be jealous."

Oh, Quent, Lyndsay thought despairingly, *why won't you admit it? Would it be so terrible to be more than friends?* She looked over at Marian, who was watching them with a knowing little smile on her face.

"I think it's time for a slower dance, don't you?" Marian said. "How about 'Stardust'? That's still my favorite."

Freddie obligingly found Marian's request, and Lyndsay turned back to Quent, who was now watching her with his jaw set and eyes that looked like embers of green fire. "Having pleasant thoughts?" she asked as his arms went around her.

"Never mind," he growled, tightening his grasp and lowering his cheek against hers. "Just be quiet and dance."

Oh, fine, Lyndsay thought. She might as well be in the arms of a grizzly bear. She closed her eyes as they shuffled slowly around the floor, more or less in rhythm to the beautiful old song. She loved the feel of Quent's cheek against hers, his breath against her ear, the strong beating of his heart, the warmth of his arms around her. If only he would whisper sweet words in her ear, this would be lovely. Instead he'd told her to be quiet and dance!

Her reverie was interrupted by a shriek from Marian, as Freddie dipped her backward, almost to the floor. "That's enough of that, young man," Marian scolded. "Now I'll probably need a massage for my back." She smiled at Lyndsay and Quent. "I do believe I'll go to bed now. I need to get back on schedule. You two can keep on dancing if you'd like."

"I think we've had enough," Quent said. "It's been a long day." He looked at Lyndsay as if seeking confirmation, but she was too annoyed with him to cooperate. She only shrugged.

"Are you two going to be party poopers, too?" Freddie asked. "It's early. We could go out and about and do a few pubs. Or if Quent's too tired, maybe Lyndsay and I . . ." He stopped, a devilish twinkle in his eyes.

Lyndsay wished she had the nerve to tell Freddie she'd go with him just to see what Quent would do, but he shot her such a dark look that she thought better of it. "No thanks, Freddie," she said. "I'm exhausted. I'm going straight up to bed. Good night."

"Come on, Quent, be a sport," Freddie persisted. "At least come into the library and have a brandy with me before you go up."

Quent hesitated for a moment, but finally agreed. Lyndsay went on up the wide staircase, smiling wryly to herself. Marian was certainly right that strong, brave men who were reticent when it came to affairs of the heart could be stirred to action by jealousy, but Quent's actions left a lot to be desired. What on earth made him keep denying something so obvious? Did he think she was an idiot?

At the door to her room, Lyndsay paused, suddenly remembering with a shiver that she'd had a couple of unpleasant experiences in there, also. *Don't be silly,* she told herself firmly. *You're acting like a nervous, suggestible nitwit again. Get your act together.* She took a deep breath and resolutely opened the door. The lights were on, and the maid had turned down her bed. It looked quite warm and cozy. Nothing to be afraid of. If she didn't look out of the window and imagine she saw something that wasn't there, she'd be just fine.

She took off her dress and hung it in the cavernous armoire, carefully removed her makeup, then put on her long cotton nightgown and got into bed. She was tempted to leave on the little bedside lamp but decided that would be cowardly and switched it off. Her fears were silly. The bed felt soft and comfortable, the mattress obviously centuries newer than the bed on which it rested. Beneath her head, the pillows were downy soft, and the bed linens were silky smooth and smelled fresh and clean. The moon was up, and shadows of the curtains moving in the breeze undulated across the ceiling like...like...

"No, they do not look like ghosts dancing," Lyndsay muttered to herself and closed her eyes. She needed to get her mind on something else. Think about Quent. Tomorrow, she and Quent were going on a picnic. That should be fun, if he forgot about Freddie and started acting human again. The abbey must be a romantic spot, the way Marian had picked up on the idea. If Quent didn't get in the mood for love, maybe she would have to lead the way. What would he do if she came right out and told him she loved him? Suddenly she held her breath and lay motionless. What was that funny noise? It sounded like something outside her window. Now it was quiet. It was probably just the wind, rustling in the ivy. *Forget it. Go to sleep.*

Lyndsay tossed and turned. Each time she almost drifted off to sleep, some little sound would jolt her wide awake. She was beginning to feel thoroughly miserable when she heard Quent's bedroom door open and close, followed by sounds of his walking across the floor. She began to relax. If Quent was close by, everything was all right. She could hear him open his armoire, the tinkle of hangers as he hung up his suit. Now he was getting undressed. That was nice to think about. Maybe sometime soon she would get to see him. She pulled her comforter closer and buried her face against her pillows. If she closed her eyes she could imagine that she and Quent were alone on a tropical shore...

IN THE NEXT ROOM, Quent hung up his suit, then tore off his shirt and underwear with impatient fingers and flung them into the laundry basket. *Damn it all,* he thought as he pulled on his pajama bottoms, *why did I have to make such a fool of myself with Lyndsay tonight?* Jealous? Of course he was jealous! He couldn't stand the sight of another man ogling her, and having her in another man's arms nearly drove him crazy. That arrogant little twerp in his fancy tuxedo! What nerve, telling him that if he didn't get moving pretty soon, he'd consider Lyndsay fair game. Even though he figured he must be Luke's main stooge in this whole affair, he had damn near taken a swing at him. They were certainly in a hurry to get him to propose to Lyndsay, but it wasn't going to work. They were pushing him too damned fast. He wasn't going to fall for that romantic setup at the abbey in the morning, either. He would go, but only as an archaeologist interested in the ruins. If Lyndsay didn't like it . . .

He sighed and shook his head. Maybe he would be able to keep his cool tomorrow, but his control was wearing awfully thin. The way she had looked tonight had pretty well destroyed what was left of it. If Freddie had just stayed out of it . . .

CHAPTER NINE

THERE WAS NOTHING but sun and sand and the whoosh-whoosh of the waves washing gently against the shore. "Lynnn-seee," a voice called. She lay beside Quent, her head nestled against his shoulder, aware only of his presence and the heat of the sun beating down on their naked bodies, and the voice calling again, "Lynnn-seee." It was getting hotter and hotter. She raised herself up and looked at Quent. "I'm too hot," she said. "Aren't you?" He looked at her and shook his head. "No, I'm not hot at all." In the distance, the voice called her name again. She squinted up at the top of the rocky cliff behind them. The cliff was so high she could barely see the man standing there, but she could tell that was where the voice came from. It called again, "Lynnn-seee, Lynnn-seee."

"I have to go now," she said.

"You'd better hurry," Quent said. "I'm leaving, too."

"I know," she said. She stood up and watched him disappear from the spot without a trace. He *would* do that, she thought as she ran across the sand toward the cliff. She found a path at the base of the cliff that angled upward in notches between the dark, jagged rocks. She kept running, up and up, her feet slipping and sliding. It was hard to breathe and her lungs felt ready to burst. She wanted to rest, but she couldn't. Something was coming after her now, something dark and shadowy. She could feel its presence, threatening to envelop her. If only Quent had stayed to help her, this wouldn't be happening. She tried to run faster, but her legs felt so heavy. It seemed as if she would never get to the top. All the time it was getting darker and darker. Now it was cold. There were thick clouds, almost on top of her. She could hear heavy breathing behind her, but when she looked back she could see nothing. At last she reached the top and raced along the edge of the cliff. The footsteps behind her were getting closer. Where was the man? "Lynnn-seee..." His voice sounded near, but she couldn't see him. It was so dark that she could barely see the edge of the cliff. The presence was almost upon her. A clammy hand touched her right arm. She tried to scream, but no sound came out, and then she was falling, falling...

Lyndsay startled violently and sat up, her heart racing. Good Lord, it was a nightmare, she thought. That was all, just a bad dream. But it had seemed so real! Even now, she felt as if the dreaded presence had followed her, was still here. She could almost believe she could hear it breathing and if she looked toward the windows she would finally see it. She looked. There *was* a man there. He wore a black cloak. He had a pale face framed by long, black hair.

Afterward, Lyndsay was never quite sure exactly what happened next. At first, she remembered feeling as if a tremendous jolt of electricity had crashed through her and her heart had stopped. She couldn't breathe. She couldn't make a sound. She felt as cold as death. Then another surge propelled her straight upward. Somehow she was on her feet, running and screaming, running away from the apparition. Desperate to escape, she wrenched open her door and ran into the hall at the same moment as Quent emerged from his room. She flung herself at him, clutching him frantically and gasping for breath, her teeth chattering.

"My God, what happened?" he said, capturing her face in his hand. "Look at me. Tell me what happened."

"Th-th-the g-g-g-ghost," she gasped. "In m-m-my r-r-room."

"You saw the ghost in your room?" His eyes scanned her face intently, but his voice was gentle, as if he were talking to a child.

Lyndsay burst into tears and nodded against his pajama front.

"What happened to Lyndsay?" Marian called as she hurried down the hall toward them.

"She saw the ghost in her room," Quent replied.

"Poor baby," Marian said, patting Lyndsay's shoulder. "I was afraid I frightened her when I told her about that. I should never have mentioned that foolishness."

"You d-didn't scare me," Lyndsay said, raising her head. "I already saw him before that. On—on the tower. I s-saw him there twice."

"Good Lord," Quent said, patting Lyndsay's back comfortingly. "Old Frederick must have decided to make friends with you."

"You're making fun of me," Lyndsay said, raising her tear-streaked face to frown at him. "You don't believe me. But I did see him. I really did."

"I believe you," Quent said. "I really do."

Lyndsay stared at him. His eyes were warm again, glowing the way they had when he saw her come down the stairs earlier. It made her feel warm again, too. She leaned against him, limp with relief.

"What's going on? Is Lyndsay all right?" It was Freddie.

"That blasted ancestor of yours just gave her a scare," Marian replied.

"Did he, now? I was just getting out of the shower when I heard Lyndsay scream. I couldn't imagine what had happened. What was the blighter doing?"

Lyndsay looked over at Freddie, who was rubbing his damp hair with a towel. "It was like a nightmare, but when I woke up he was standing there looking at me," she said. "I heard someone calling my name in my dream, and when I opened my eyes, there he was."

"I'll be damned," Freddie said. "He hasn't been around in a long time. How's the old fellow looking these days?"

Lyndsay stared at Freddie resentfully, but said nothing. It was plain he didn't believe her, either.

"I don't think Lyndsay's in any mood to joke about it," Quent said.

"And I don't blame her," Marian put in. "Freddie, why don't you be brave and go into her room and see if there's something there?"

"Right-o," Freddie said. He disappeared into Lyndsay's room and came back a few moments later. "Clean as a whistle," he said. "No sign of breaking and entering."

"I'm not going back in there," Lyndsay said. As a matter of fact, she would just as soon spend the night standing in the hall in Quent's arms. She loved the feeling of being so close to him with only their night clothes between them.

"Maybe you two could exchange rooms," Marian suggested. "Would that make you feel better, dear?"

"I—I guess so," Lyndsay replied doubtfully. She wasn't sure she'd feel safe from ghostly visitations anywhere in Gravelpick Manor, but she didn't want to cause more disruptions. As it was, everyone already thought she was crazy.

"I know something that'll help even more," Freddie said. "Come with me." He led the way into Quent's room and opened the door of the huge armoire against the wall next to Lyndsay's room. "Let's see if I remember," he said, frowning and reaching inside it. "Oh, yes. There we go." He stepped inside the armoire and pushed Quent's clothing aside, revealing that he could go through to the armoire in Lyndsay's room, which he proceeded to do, opening those doors and providing a passageway between the two rooms. "This old place is full of tricks," he said, returning with a broad smile on his face. "Secret passages all over. Now, if you need Quent, he can reach you in a jiffy."

"Imagine that," said Marian. "I never even knew it was there."

"I could show you a dozen more," Freddie said. "Well, back to bed." He gave Quent a broad wink. "Don't say I never did you any favors."

"If you're sure you'll be all right, I'll run along, too," Marian said.

"I'll be fine," Lyndsay said. "I'm awfully sorry I bothered everyone."

"No bother," Marian said with a smile. "People with ghosts in their houses have to expect such things."

"Are you sure you're all right?" Quent asked when the others had gone, surveying Lyndsay's face with a worried frown. "You still look a little anxious."

"I guess I am," Lyndsay said, "but mostly I feel stupid. Or am I crazy? I can tell everyone thinks I just imagined something."

"It doesn't matter how it happened," Quent said. "I don't like to see you so frightened. When I first touched you, you were as cold as ice." He reached over and felt Lyndsay's bare arm. "You're still chilly. Don't you have a warmer nightgown?" His eyes wandered down Lyndsay's form, and she was suddenly aware that her thin nightie was a lot more revealing than the dress she had worn to dinner. She clutched her arms about herself.

"I was fine when I was in bed. Too warm," she said. "I think that's what started my nightmare."

"Then you'd better get back to bed," Quent said. "Do you want to stay in here?"

Lyndsay glanced over at Quent's bed. She could see what he had meant about the carved lions. They perched on each bedpost, and a huge lion's head was carved into the headboard. "I guess maybe those lions would protect me," she said, managing a weak smile.

"Probably so," Quent said. "It might help if you left a light on, too. And we'll leave the doorway between open. You can call me if you need me."

"Yes. I'll do that," Lyndsay said. She tried to smile at Quent, but her lips trembled and she felt a dull, lonely ache inside. There he stood, tall and broad-shouldered in his dark blue pajamas, his eyes warm and concerned. How she loved him. He was so kind and gentle. He would always be there to take care of her. She wished he would offer to stay with her, but she knew he wouldn't, because he wasn't that kind of a man. Instead, he would quietly go into the other room and go to sleep. A tear trickled down her cheek. She didn't want him to go. She wanted him to hold her in his arms.

"What is it, Lyndsay?" Quent asked seeing the tear. "Are you still that frightened?"

Lyndsay shook her head. "No," she said hoarsely, but another tear followed, and another.

Quent put his arms around her and patted her back comfortingly. "You are still frightened," he said. "Tell me what I can do to make you feel better. Would you like a drink of some kind?"

"N-no," Lyndsay choked out in the midst of a rush of tears brought on by Quent's soft, sympathetic voice. "Just hold me." She put her arms around him and clung to him, and felt his arms tighten around her. He was so big and warm and strong. He smelled so clean and masculine. She wanted to stay close and never let him go.

"I think you're worn out," Quent said near her ear. "You haven't had a chance to get used to the time change yet, and you got that nasty bump on your head besides. It's been a long, hard day for you. Put your arms around my neck and I'll tuck you into bed." Lyndsay complied, burying her face in Quent's neck as he carried her to the bed and then leaned over and set her upon it. "You can let go now," he said, giving her a little smile.

Lyndsay shook her head and laced her fingers together behind his neck. "Don't go," she said. "Stay here." His face was so close to hers that she could see a flash of something very near to panic in his eyes before he covered it with a frown.

"I can't do that, Lyndsay," he said. "Please let go."

"Why can't you?" she asked, ignoring his request.

"Damn it, Lyndsay," he growled, "you're a grown woman. You know why I can't. Let go."

"Tell me why," she said stubbornly. She could see a flush come to Quent's cheeks. A bright, hidden fire suddenly burst forth in his eyes and sent an answering rush of excitement through her. So he wasn't as calm as he pretended!

"Because it's driving me crazy, seeing you in that nightgown." He reached back and pulled her hands apart. "That's enough now. Go to sleep." He turned and started to walk away.

"Coward!" Lyndsay shot after him. "You won't even kiss me good-night."

Quent stopped and whirled around, glaring. "I am not a coward. I'm thinking of you. Under the circumstances, I might not want to stop at a kiss. I might not be able to."

"Only might not? Then you are a coward," Lyndsay goaded. She could feel the current flowing between them now and her heart beat faster. "I should have guessed, since the only time I can get anything like passion from you is when you're too exhausted to know what you're doing, or you think I'm dead."

Quent took several steps back toward her. "There is nothing wrong with having self-control," he said in a voice harsh with strain. "If all you want is sex, that's easy enough to arrange, but it takes time to establish a lasting relationship between two people. I was hoping you were more interested in that sort of thing."

"I am," Lyndsay snapped, "but that doesn't mean I want to just hold hands while I get old and gray. You could have a lasting relationship with a car that just sits in the garage, but if its engine won't run when you finally try it it's not worth very much."

"That is not the same thing!" Quent roared. "It's ridiculous to compare—" He stopped suddenly, staring blankly at Lyndsay. Then a smile spread slowly across his face. "That was a very clever analogy," he said. "Somehow I never thought of you as a car, though. All right, I'll stay, for a little while."

Lyndsay said nothing. She felt so triumphant that she didn't dare. Instead, she smiled and slid farther onto the bed and patted the space beside her. Quent came to her, tucked the covers over her, then sat down. He put one hand on either side of her and leaned toward her. Lyndsay put her arms around his neck and pulled him closer.

"We shouldn't be doing this," he said, but the glow in his eyes gave him away.

Lyndsay smiled and touched his lips with her fingertip. "Yes, we should," she whispered, then sighed contentedly as his lips found hers. This time she was absolutely sure Quent knew what he was doing.

The passion of his kiss was everything Lyndsay could have wanted and more. From the terror of only a short time before she felt as if she were being borne on a soft, warm cloud into a heaven filled with dazzling colors. While their mouths exchanged sweet secrets, Quent's arms found their way beneath her to hold her close, and Lyndsay's hands slipped into the thick silkiness of his hair, loving the way it felt, so cool and clean. Rather than crush her with his weight, he stretched out beside her and held her against him, one hand gently caressing her back. His kisses explored her face, her neck, her ears. Slowly, the blanket between them was pushed away, and Lyndsay could feel the warmth of Quent's body against hers, the steely strength of his muscular legs against her thighs. She could tell he wanted her, and she held her breath as he molded her against him. She knew he didn't want to stop. Would he be able to? Did she want him to go on? Her body left no doubt of its answer, waves of desire winging through her with the wild disarray of a flight of startled birds as Quent's hands gently explored her soft curves while his lips nibbled delicately at hers. No answer came to her dazed mind and she moved against him, sighing deeply.

All at once, Quent's body tensed. He released Lyndsay and rolled from the bed in one swift motion. "I think we'd better stop," he said gruffly as he reached down and pulled the blanket back over Lyndsay.

Lyndsay stared at him. He didn't look angry, only frustrated, which was certainly the way she felt, the warmth of seconds ago replaced by an empty ache. "I suppose so," she said without enthusiasm.

Quent cocked his head and studied her. "Only suppose so?" he asked. "Have you considered the, uh, possible consequences if we don't?"

"Possible consequences?" Lyndsay's mind darted about. At first she could think of nothing terrible that might happen. Then suddenly she realized what Quent was driving at and her eyes widened. "You mean a baby?" she asked, her cheeks growing warm.

Quent shook his head and sighed, his expression like that of a disappointed and worried parent. "For a minute there I thought I was going to have to explain the birds and bees to you," he said. "I hope you haven't been going through life with such abandoned disregard for the facts of life. You're lucky you haven't suffered the consequences if you have."

Quent's words sent a shock wave crackling through Lyndsay's brain that cleared out the cobwebs in an instant. She sat up, clutching the blanket around her. "If you're insinuating that you think I may have been promiscuous, you are way, way off," she said, glaring at him. "I most definitely haven't, and I wouldn't! If you don't know me any better than that by now, you're an idiot!"

There was silence for several seconds. Quent lifted one hand and covered his eyes, then rubbed it back and forth as if his forehead hurt. Lyndsay watched him anxiously. His mouth was working strangely. Didn't he believe her?

When she asked him he lowered his hand and burst out laughing.

"Of course I believe you," he said.

"I don't think it's funny," Lyndsay said sulkily.

Quent sat down beside her again and took her face between his hands. "I'm sorry. I wasn't laughing at you, I was laughing at the way our communications get garbled. It's as much my fault as it is yours." He put his arms around her and held her close, burying his cheek in her hair. "I worry about you too much, I guess," he said softly. "I can't help it. I—" his voice broke as he went on "—I care so much about you."

Tears pricked at Lyndsay's eyes and a warm glow filled her heart. That time, Quent had almost said he loved her. She could feel it deep inside. "I care about you, too," she whispered.

"That's good to hear." Quent drew back and smiled, his eyes misty. "Good night, Lyndsay," he said. "Sleep well. Don't worry about anything. No ghosts or goblins or things that go bump in the night? All right?"

Lyndsay shook her head. "I won't. I'll be fine."

"Good." Quent kissed her lips softly. "See you in the morning."

He got up and ducked swiftly through the open armoire without a backward glance. Lyndsay watched his broad shoulders disappear, the warmth of his embrace still with her, a little fire of hope burning fiercely in her heart. She loved him so. In just one day they'd made a lot of progress. Maybe it wouldn't be so long, after all, before he was ready to say he loved her, too. Maybe tomorrow at the abbey...

QUENT WENT into Lyndsay's room and then stood looking down at her bed. He did not, he thought ruefully, feel much like sleeping. Another day like this one and he was going to be a basket case, and so was Lyndsay. Poor little love had been so terrified, and then so absolutely irresistible. He should have said no, but damn it all, he wasn't made of steel.

He walked over to the window and leaned out to look up at the tower. Lyndsay said she'd seen the ghost up there earlier, even though she denied it this morning. She must have been embarrassed to admit being so suggestible. There certainly wasn't anything there now that even vaguely resembled a ghost. He pulled in his head and was about to turn around when something on the window ledge caught his eye. It looked like a crushed ivy leaf. He picked it up, then stuck his head out of the window again, this time examining the wall below the window. "Well, I'll be damned," he said aloud, reaching out to feel the rope that was embedded in the vines below the window and anchored to a metal spike of some sort driven between the stones. So that was it. Someone, doubtless Freddie, had climbed up the wall and into Lyndsay's room, scared the living daylights out of her, then vanished into one of those secret passages he knew. That young man, Quent vowed grimly, was going to have a lot of questions to answer in the morning.

He went and sat on the edge of the bed, his jaw clenched in anger. This plot of Luke's was getting out of hand, and he'd had just about enough of it. There was no way he was going to put up with being manipulated like a puppet and having his Lyndsay terrorized day and night. Poor baby, she apparently didn't have anything to do with it, after all. Her description of Gravelpick Manor had been just a lucky guess. Dozens of English castles probably answered similar descriptions.

He got to his feet and began pacing around the room. What should they do? There was nothing he'd like better right now than to go home. Of course, he'd have to be absolutely sure first there was no real reason to stay, but he'd bet all of his detective's instincts that there was none. He slammed his fist against his hand and sat down again, his mind made up. In the morning he would get the truth out of Freddie, one way or another, tell Marian the game was over, and then make reservations to leave. He doubted Lyndsay would be unhappy over his decision, after today, especially when she found out what Luke and Theresa had been up to. Then, when they were home—he got into bed and stretched luxuriously—he would think about getting Lyndsay a ring sometime very soon.

CHAPTER TEN

WHEN LYNDSAY AWOKE, she discovered it was ten o'clock, and a quick peek into what was now Quent's room disclosed he was already gone. He could at least have wakened her with a kiss, Lyndsay thought with a sigh. He must have had to tiptoe through his room to get his shaving things from the bath, for they were gone. She dressed quickly and went down to the breakfast room. To her surprise, Marian was still sitting there drinking coffee, a rather anxious look on her face.

"Good morning," Lyndsay greeted her. "You look worried. Are some of your roses not doing well?"

"Oh, they're fine," Marian replied. "It's Quent." She pursed her mouth and shook her head. "He said he didn't want to go to the abbey today, after all, and that he wanted to have a talk with me later. Then he went off, looking for Freddie. I can't think what's wrong, unless he resents our attempts to bring you two together. Did he seem upset last night?"

"Not at all," Lyndsay replied, her heart sinking. "That's just like him, though. Just when I think everything's going well, he backs off." But this, she thought grimly, sounded more serious than usual.

"Oh, dear." Marian sighed. "Well, I'll apologize if that's what it is, and try to be more subtle in the future. Are you ready for breakfast, dear?"

"I guess so," Lyndsay replied, although her appetite seemed suddenly to have vanished.

"I'll tell Cook on my way out," Marian said. "I've got to see to some business. Do let me know if you find out anything."

"I will," Lyndsay agreed. Darn, she thought angrily. What on earth had gotten into Quent now? Here it was, a beautiful day, and now he didn't want to go to the abbey. "I've had all I can take," she muttered. That man was going to answer some questions this morning, and if she didn't get some straight answers, she was through waiting around for him to resolve whatever conflicts he still had.

That decided, she picked up the North Twickham newspaper, which Marian had left on the table. It was a typical small-town paper, the news consisting of such events as club meetings and wedding announcements, and the exciting item that Constable Barnwell had almost caught up with some men suspected of smuggling arms to Northern Ireland. He had a tip-off on a cache of weapons, but when he got there it was gone. Poor old fellow, Lyndsay thought. His luck was running like hers. Just think you've got something exciting, and poof! it isn't there, after all.

"Too bad you aren't going to the abbey today," the cook said when she brought Lyndsay's breakfast. "It's so lovely out."

"I know," Lyndsay said. "I wish we were going." She did her best to do justice to the food, but finally gave up. There was no point in trying to make her churning stomach digest anything. She got up and walked slowly down the ancestral hallway, her hands thrust into the pockets of her slacks, a dark frown on her face.

She had just reached the foyer when Quent came in the door, wearing a smug, self-satisfied look. When he saw Lyndsay, he smiled, but it was not, she noticed, an affectionate smile. It only added to his self-congratulatory look. "You seem very pleased with yourself," she said coolly. "Did you find Freddie?"

"I did," Quent replied. "He was busy fixing the carburetor on one of the old farm trucks and didn't want to take time to talk, but when I told him I'd break him in half if he didn't he talked plenty. Let's go in the library and I'll tell you about it." He walked swiftly in that direction without even looking to see if Lyndsay was following, an omission that only added to her displeasure.

So what if he had warned Freddie off, she thought. Was she supposed to give him a medal for that? She did follow, thinking as she did so that she didn't give a darn for hearing a blow-by-blow description of his talk with Freddie. She wanted to know why they weren't going to the abbey. As soon as they were inside the huge room she said, "Before you start, I want to know why we're not going to the abbey today."

Quent sat in one of the chairs next to the long table and gestured to the next chair. "Sit down and I'll tell you all about it," he said, giving her what she thought was an infuriatingly bland smile, like a tolerant parent about to explain why they couldn't go to the zoo, after all.

"No thanks, I'll stand," she said icily. "This had better be good."

For a moment, Quent looked taken aback, then he nodded. "Very well. First of all, I should tell you that when I went into your room last night, I discovered who your ghost was. It was Freddie. He climbed up a rope that's buried beneath the ivy, one that he now tells me he put there when he was a teenager.'' He paused and raised his eyebrows meaningfully at Lyndsay.

"That's interesting," Lyndsay said, thinking of her speculations on that possibility from the rose garden. "At least now I know I wasn't crazy. So what?"

"So what?" Quent frowned. "Frankly, I don't understand your attitude. I think it was inexcusable, frightening you like that. But that isn't all." His eyes narrowed. "Freddie also confirmed what I've suspected for some time. Our trip here has nothing to do with any detective work. It's all a scam, cooked up by Luke Thorndike and my sister to try to, uh, further our relationship. Oh, Alfred was looking for someone to be a companion to Marian on the flight back and while he was gone, but she doesn't need protecting. She's supposed to use her matchmaking skills to the utmost while Freddie does his bit to make me jealous and also impersonates the Gravelpick ghost so you'll come running to me for protection." His eyes flashed. "I strongly object to being manipulated like that, and I have no intention of staying around to play nursemaid to Marian. I have better things to do with my time. We're going home immediately, and when we get there, Luke and Theresa are really going to hear from me."

Stunned, Lyndsay sank into the chair Quent had pulled out for her. He was so upset by being what he called manipulated that he didn't even care that it had brought them closer. He had threatened Freddie, and, from what Marian had said, he intended to bawl her out, too! Suddenly she was so angry that she thought she'd explode. She jumped to her feet, glaring at Quent.

"That does it!" she snapped. "You're so afraid something might really happen between us that you can't stand it, can you? I've been manipulated just as much as you have, and I don't want to go home. In fact, I'm not going! I'll stay and keep Marian company, and when Sir Alfred gets back I may go on to France or something. One thing's for sure, I'm not going back to work for you." She whirled and started for the door.

"Lyndsay, wait!" Quent called after her. "I didn't think—"

"You certainly didn't!" Lyndsay interrupted, stopping long enough to glare at him again. When he started toward her, she held up her hand. "Don't come near me. And don't you dare give Marian any trouble, or I'll pay you back somehow, I swear I will."

Quent shook his head. "I won't. Where are you going?"

"Out," Lyndsay said. She gave Quent a nasty, witchlike smile. "I think I may look for Freddie. Maybe I do like him, after all."

With that, she ran out of the house, down the steps and along the road toward the barns. As she ran, tears began to stream down her cheeks. Quent didn't love her. He was so afraid of love and commitment that he latched on to the slightest excuse to run away. Manipulated! If anyone had been manipulated, she had. She'd gotten her hopes up, only to have them dashed to smithereens. Darn Theresa, anyway! It was probably her idea. Just because Luke had tricked her with that silly assassination plot, she thought something like that would work with Quent. She should have known her brother better than that.

Short of breath, Lyndsay slowed down and looked back over her shoulder. There was no sign of Quent following her. She might have guessed that, too! She dashed the tears from her cheeks and started running again. At the drive that led to the barn where the bicycles were kept, she slowed, then turned in. She didn't really want to see

Freddie, or anyone else. This was a good time to ride around for a while and see more of the Gravelpick lands while she got herself under control. How could she bear to face Quent again and know that none of her dreams would ever come true? That thought brought another flood of tears, and she had to stop and wipe her eyes and blow her nose.

She located the blue bike and rode off, this time taking the fork left where she and Quent had turned right before. The road led past the maintenance barn, but there was no one there now. It followed a small stream for half a mile or so, crossed it on an ancient stone bridge, then climbed a small hill between a hayfield and a pasture, where a small herd of cattle grazed peacefully. Lyndsay stopped and got off the bike at the top of the hill, sitting down on the stone pasture fence to think, a miserable ache in her heart. Had she been too hasty? she wondered. Was it reasonable for Quent to have been so upset? Theresa, she knew, had been furious at first when she found out what Luke was up to.

"What do you think?" Lyndsay said to a black, white-faced cow that had stopped grazing and was staring at her. "Should I go back and try to straighten things out?"

The cow flipped its ears and went back to grazing.

"Was that a yes or no?" Lyndsay asked. Probably a "you figure it out" she decided with a sigh. She leaned her chin on her hand and stared into the distance.

On the other side of the little hill the road faded into nothing more than a cow path. About a hundred yards away, partially concealed by a lone oak tree beside the path, the sides and battered roof of a small stone building could be seen. It looked like the old ruin Alfred described, Lyndsay thought. She decided to go and have a look at it while she figured out what to do. There was no point in hurrying back to the house. It would be better to give Quent a chance to think, too.

Lyndsay got back on her bike and coasted slowly down the hill. As she drew nearer the building, she occasionally caught the sound of men's voices. Funny, she thought. Freddie had made it sound as if no one ever went there. The path grew steeper and bumpier, and she got off of her bike again and walked it along. She had just reached the oak tree when the men's voices became louder. She could plainly hear "Careful! ... I've got it.... Damn, this is heavy."

Curious, she leaned her bike against the tree and moved slowly forward along the side of the building. When she reached the corner, she peeked around, then quickly drew back, her heart racing. Parked with its back to the building was an old blue pickup, and standing in the back of the truck, helping two heavyset men push a long wooden box forward in the truck bed on top of a pile of others like it, was Freddie Frobisher. She had seen boxes like that in an exhibit of contraband items seized by the U.S. border patrol. They were munitions boxes. The news item about Constable Barnwell's missing arms cache flashed into her mind and suddenly connected. "Good Lord," she muttered. Freddie might not be a threat to Marian, but he was involved with illegal shipments of arms. He was a threat to a great many people!

Feeling as if she were holding her breath in an attempt to make no sound, Lyndsay tried desperately to think what to do. She was, she knew, in a dangerous situation. Those men were not playing games, they were playing for keeps, and if they caught her snooping she might not have long to live. They were busy now, making plenty of noise. She might be able to sneak back the way she had come before they finished loading the truck. Surely they weren't going to drive up the road she had come down, carrying munitions boxes out in plain sight.

"That's enough for this load," came the sound of Freddie's voice. "We have to leave room for the hay to cover the boxes."

They were going up the road! Lyndsay's heart began to pound harder. Even if she could hide, they would see her bike by the tree. It was practically on the road. She had to get out of here, and fast. She slipped back along the building, took hold of her bicycle, and had just gotten it turned around when a voice behind her said, "Hold it right there, Lyndsay. Let go of the bike and turn around slowly."

Lyndsay did as instructed. Standing at the corner of the building was Freddie, and in his hand was a heavy black revolver. "Wh-why, hello, Freddie," she said, trying to smile at him. "What are you doing here? Why are you pointing a gun at me?"

"Because you're someplace you shouldn't be," he said coolly. "I tried to tell you to stay away from here, but you didn't listen. Now put your hands behind your head and come on down here. Right now." When she reached him he frisked her, then pushed her in front of him. "Good girl. Just keep going."

Good Lord, Lyndsay thought numbly as she went ahead of Freddie into the dank interior of the old ruined building, everything was going wrong today.

"What are you going to do with her? Shoot her?" asked one of the men.

"Eventually," Freddie replied. "I'm going to tie her up in the cellar for now. Cover her while I go down the ladder, then when she's down, you follow." He went to an open trapdoor, turned and let himself down into the hole. "I'm down," he called.

The man brandished a semiautomatic rifle at Lyndsay. "Go on," he snarled.

A feeling of dread settled into Lyndsay's stomach. She was overmatched. There was nothing she could do. She let herself through the opening, into a dark, dank cellar. The man followed.

"Why don't you let me get rid of her now?" he asked. "Someone might come looking for her."

"That's what I'm counting on," said Freddie. "She's got a boyfriend. We'll put both of them under the next load and get rid of them somewhere far away. The last thing we need is a lot of blood around here to make people ask questions." He poked his gun into Lyndsay's ribs. "Sit down in that chair and put your hands behind it," he said.

There was an old rickety chair near a table that sat against the far wall. Lyndsay sat.

"Hold your gun on her while I tie her up," Freddie said to the man.

He tells that man every move to make just like Quent does me sometimes, Lyndsay thought. Thinking about Quent made another surge of misery course through her. She might never see him again.

The man bent and peered into Lyndsay's face as Freddie tied her wrists together behind the chair. "Pretty little piece, isn't she? Why don't we have a little fun with her before we go?"

Freddie finished tying Lyndsay's wrists together, then stood up and without warning gave the man a vicious hit across the mouth with the edge of his hand. "Shut up, you jackass," he said. "You two hurry up and get that damned hay loaded now and get the hell out of here. We're on a precise schedule, or had you lamebrains forgotten that?"

The man gave Freddie a resentful look and went back up the ladder.

Freddie brought more rope and began to tie Lyndsay more securely to the chair so that even her feet couldn't move. "Sorry to have to do this," he said, grinning wickedly at her, "but I wouldn't want you to run off."

Lyndsay glared at him but said nothing, trying to fight off a rising tide of panic. *Keep your mind busy,* she told herself. *Look for something to help you if you get a chance.* She cast her gaze around the small room, which she estimated to be about ten by fifteen feet. Out of the corner of her eye she could see the table behind her. On it, a small oil lamp flickered dimly. The wall to her left was the catacomb Alfred had mentioned, except that the niches did not look large enough for human remains. To her right, near the ladder, was another pile of munitions boxes. The right wall contained more niches, even smaller.

"Those catacomb niches don't look big enough for human bodies," she mused aloud. "Maybe this was a pet cemetery."

Freddie looked up at her and laughed. "That's the best theory I've heard yet." He finished his knot tying and stood up. "How does it happen that someone who screams bloody murder when a ghost appears is so calm when they're in real danger?"

Lyndsay frowned thoughtfully. "I don't know. This is different." But it was odd, she thought. Her mind seemed strangely detached from her body.

"That it is," Freddie agreed. He laughed again. "The way you screamed when I did that little act in your bedroom, I thought you really might wake the dead."

Lyndsay glared at him again. "If I'd known it was you, you wouldn't be here now," she snapped. "You're a...a monster."

Freddie made an exaggerated pout. "Such ingratitude. And after I risked life and limb climbing up that old rope just to give your love life a little boost. You can't deny that Quent needed a little shove in the right direction, can you? And it did get him moving for a while, didn't it?"

Lyndsay pursed her mouth and looked away. It had done more harm than good. Clever detective that he was, Quent had discovered the rope and confirmed what had apparently before been only suspicions. There was a shout from above that the hay was loaded. Freddie scurried up the ladder. For a few minutes, Lyndsay thought Freddie was going to go off and leave her there, and that if he did and Quent came looking for her she would be saved. She heard the truck start and her glimmer of hope grew stronger, but almost immediately Freddie returned.

"Now we wait for Quent," he said, sitting down on one of the remaining munitions boxes.

"I doubt if he'll show up at all," Lyndsay said. "We had a fight." If Freddie was on a tight schedule, that might worry him.

"Did you, now?" Freddie said. "What about?"

"None of your business," Lyndsay said coldly.

"Tch, tch, a lovers' quarrel," Freddie clucked. "Apparently he's got over it. When I called him on my cellular phone and told him to come on down here and give me a hand getting you up the ladder, because you've sprained your ankle, he said he'd be here in a jiffy."

"He'd do that, anyway," Lyndsay said, her heart sinking. Much as she wanted to see Quent, she did not want him in this miserable situation with her. She fought back a sudden wave of nausea and panic. When Quent got there she had to be able to think fast. With any chance at all, Quent was more than a match for Freddie alone.

"I suppose you're right about that," Freddie said. "He's the very epitome of the American straight-arrow hero. Virtuous to a fault but dull."

"He is not dull!" Lyndsay snapped. "Being serious and thoughtful and kind and considerate is not being dull, but you wouldn't understand about that."

Freddie got up and came toward her, smiling. "I know you love him. I wonder if he has any idea how lucky he is?"

Lyndsay said nothing. She wanted to be able to listen for the slightest sound outside that would tell her Quent was coming, so she could warn him. That hope was quickly dashed. Freddie pulled a handkerchief out of his jacket pocket and wadded it into a ball.

"I'm afraid I'm going to have to make sure you don't try to warn Quent," he said. "This handkerchief's clean. Open your mouth, and don't try to bite me. Remember who has the gun."

"No," Lyndsay said and then clenched her teeth as tightly as she could. The very idea of having her mouth stuffed full of Freddie's handkerchief clean or not, revolted her. Freddie slapped her face roughly several times, but she did not exclaim in pain and give him the opportunity he sought. She only closed her eyes and gritted her teeth even harder.

"Stubborn, aren't you?" Freddie said. "Very well, I'll use the tape without it, but you won't like it any better." He took a roll of duct tape from the table and wound it tightly around Lyndsay's mouth several times. "That ought to keep you pretty quiet," he said.

Lyndsay's eyes shot flashes of hatred toward him. Good Lord, but he was loathsome.

"I can see I'm not making much of a hit with you," Freddie said with a whimsical smile. "I do wish I didn't have to do this, but it's absolutely necessary. I've got a lot of time invested in seeing that this caper comes out right, and a lot of people are depending on me. I can't let a couple of snoopy American private investigators spoil it at the last minute." When Lyndsay's eyes widened he grinned. "Surprised you, didn't I? I've known all along that you and Quent weren't archaeologists. I heard the whole story Uncle Alfie gave you. He didn't tell Aunt Marian, though. He was afraid she might slip up and give everything away, so all she knew was that she was supposed to play matchmaker for a pair of archaeologists. She didn't even know that was me last night. I suppose Quent will tell her, though, and then I'll be on her blacklist for a while."

That, Lyndsay thought, would suit her just fine.

Freddie glanced at his watch and then fell silent. Moments later, the roar of a motorbike could be heard coming closer.

"There he comes," Freddie said. "I told him to bring that old trail bike I've been using." He got up and stood behind Lyndsay, holding his gun against the base of her skull. "Just keep quiet and you'll be all right," he said softly. "One sound and I'll pull the trigger."

There was the sound of footsteps entering the building and then walking over to the trapdoor. Quent's voice called, "Lyndsay? Freddie?"

"Come on down the ladder," Freddie called back.

Lyndsay's heart began to pound as Quent started down the ladder. She loved him so. She could bear anything that might happen to her, but to have Quent murdered in cold blood just because she had stupidly gotten angry and run off.... A convulsive sob shook her and came out as a croaking noise.

Quent had just reached the floor. He whirled around and looked toward the sound. Coming in from the light, he squinted into the semidarkness. His eyes fell on Lyndsay and Freddie and he stared at them for a moment, dumbstruck, then started toward them. "Damn it, Freddie," he snarled. "I told you I've had enough of your games."

"This is no game, old chap," Freddie replied. "Stop right there or Lyndsay's dead."

Quent stopped. His eyes met Lyndsay's. *Oh, Quent,* she thought, her heart pounding erratically. *I love you, I love you, I love you. Please don't do anything foolish.* She thought she saw an answering flicker of understanding, but in the dim light she couldn't be sure. She held her breath as his eyes flashed around the room in what, Lyndsay knew, was a futile attempt to find some way out of this miserable situation. She also knew he would find none. Freddie could pull the trigger faster than Quent could make any move to free her. At last Quent's eyes fell on the pile of munitions boxes. "So that's it," he said, his face grim.

"I see you've got the picture," Freddie said. "I want you to put your hands behind you, walk over to me, then turn your back." When Quent had done what he told him to, Freddie expertly put a pair of handcuffs on his wrists, then gave him a kick that sent him sprawling. As quickly as a cowboy roping a steer, Freddie leaped forward and tied Quent's ankles together, then bound his wrists and ankles behind him. "That ought to hold you," he said. "You two have a nice chat. I've got some business to attend to. I'll be back to take care of you later." With that, he hurried up the ladder, pulled it up after him, and closed the trapdoor behind him. In moments there came the sound of a car starting up and driving off.

Seeing Quent lying bound on the floor suddenly brought home to Lyndsay the enormity of their problem and a fresh wave of nausea swept through her. Trembling, she fought it back, watching as Quent maneuvered himself onto his side and then into a position where he could see her.

"Are you all right?" he asked. "Did Freddie . . . ?"

Lyndsay shook her head.

"Thank God," Quent said fervently. "When I get my hands on that guy. . . It's all my fault we're in this mess. If I weren't such a fool. . ." He stopped as another sob racked Lyndsay's chest. "Don't cry, sweetheart," he said gently. "I swear to God, we'll get out of this somehow. Let's be very calm and figure out how to get loose before Freddie comes back. There doesn't seem to be much slack in my ropes, but I'll see if I can loosen anything."

For several seconds, Lyndsay watched as Quent silently tried to work his hands and feet free, her heart aching and glowing at the same time. He was so strong and good. And he had called her sweetheart. . . .

"I can't seem to find anything to get hold of," he said at last. "I'm going to move over behind you now and see what your knots look like. Have you tried to free your hands?"

Lyndsay nodded.

"No luck, then. Here I go." Quent writhed and maneuvered himself across the floor until his head was behind Lyndsay's chair. "If you were down where I could reach you, I think I could get you loose," he said. "Try and tip your chair over toward me so you'll land on me and won't get hurt."

Lyndsay jerked her body as hard as she could in Quent's direction, but the old chair only creaked and stayed upright. She tried again and again, but the chair, sunken into the dirt floor, would not fall. The hope she had felt minutes before faded into despair. They were doomed. She groaned and shook her head.

"Don't give up, sweetheart," Quent said. "We aren't through yet. I'm going to try getting up on my knees and then throwing my weight against the chair. Hang on."

Quent struggled to his knees, then launched himself sideways at the chair. The chair gave way with a crack, its legs splintering from the impact. Lyndsay felt herself falling, but she also felt her ropes loosening. When she came to rest, her legs were free, only the top part of her body still attached to the chair back.

She made as triumphant a sound as she could under the circumstances, then pushed herself against Quent's back, her hands touching his.

"Now we're getting somewhere," he said, squeezing her fingers between his, "but first I want to say something. I love you, Lyndsay. I'll always love you. And if you can forgive all my shortcomings, when we get out of this mess, I want to marry you."

At the same time as Quent said those words, his heart was pounding in his chest. They were, he knew only too well, in a worse situation than he had ever been in his life, and it was his fault. If he had thought about Lyndsay before, instead of himself, told her he loved her when he knew he did, this would never have happened. It was a mistake he would never make again. Now it was up to him to keep calm and get them out of here safely. He would do it, or die trying.

CHAPTER ELEVEN

LYNDSAY COULD scarcely believe what she had heard Quent say. Here they were, lying back-to-back on the filthy dirt floor of a centuries-old ruin, their lives in danger of being snuffed out at any moment, and Quent had suddenly decided to tell her he loved her and wanted to marry her. What a man, she thought. She nodded her head, made mmm-hmm sounds and squeezed his fingers as tightly as she could in return.

"Was that a yes?" he asked.

Lyndsay nodded and made more positive sounds.

Quent chuckled. "That's all the extra motivation I need, although I wouldn't have blamed you if you'd said no." As he manipulated the ropes he went on, "Any woman in her right mind could be excused for turning down a man who's such a fool that he resents it if someone tricks the woman he adores into throwing herself into his arms. I've almost got it. Move down a little... There we go. Can you get your hands free now?"

Lyndsay pulled her hands free, then sat up and tore the tape from her mouth. "There! I'm free!" she cried. "Except for this stuff around my chest." She quickly unwound it, then turned toward Quent and put her face down close to his. "I love you, Quent," she said, "and I'm going to kiss you while you still can't get away from me." She kissed his lips lingeringly, then pulled back and smiled at him.

He smiled back at her, the glow from his eyes so strong and warm that Lyndsay had the sensation that they warmed and illuminated the whole cellar. "I wouldn't mind if you kept me tied up and kissed me like that for days at a time," he said, "but I think we'd better concentrate on getting out of here first."

Lyndsay nodded, suddenly remembering that Quent knew nothing about the other men who might return. While she undid his ropes she told him what she had seen and heard when she'd first arrived. "There!" she said at last. "Now you can stand up." She helped him to his feet. "What can we do about those handcuffs?"

"Not much right now, I'm afraid," Quent replied. "I don't see any tools lying about. Let's get out of here and find some."

"But Freddie pulled the ladder up after him," Lyndsay said, looking toward the faint light that showed through the cracks of the trapdoor.

"No problem," Quent said. "I think you can reach the door from my shoulders." He crouched down. "Hop on. It's piggyback time."

Quent was right—Lyndsay could reach the trapdoor. She had just gotten half of the door open when the unmistakable sound of an automobile approaching on a bumpy road came to their ears. "Oh, no," she said, "what do we do now? Freddie's coming back."

"Open the other half, quickly, then get back down." Lyndsay did so, then Quent crouched and she climbed off of his shoulders. They could hear the car stop outside. "I'm going to get where I can knock the ladder out from under him if he comes down." Quent whispered. "You grab one of the old chair legs and go and hide behind the pile of boxes and be ready to bash him. He may think we've already gone, and go away."

The seconds seemed like hours to Lyndsay as she crouched behind the munitions boxes. They heard the car door slam shut, then footsteps coming into the building, then the sound of the Freddie swearing volubly as he saw the open trapdoor. Apparently unable to believe that his quarry had escaped, he put the ladder down through the trapdoor opening. Lyndsay waited, listening intently to the sound of him stepping on the first rung, then the second, the third, the fourth . . .

The sound of the fifth step never came. Instead, she heard the pounding of Quent's footsteps as he gave himself a short running start, and the thud of his shoulder hitting the ladder. She stood up in time to hear Freddie's howl of surprise and to see him go flying backward, catapulted across the room. She leaped forward, ready to wield her weapon, but there was no need. He landed off balance and fell backward, hitting his head against the edge of the old table. He crumpled to the floor, unconscious.

"Is he dead?" Lyndsay asked, looking down at Freddie as Quent came to her side.

"I doubt it," Quent said. "Get his gun and see if the keys to these handcuffs are in his pockets."

Lyndsay found both items quickly. She unlocked the handcuffs, then gave Quent the gun and a handful of ammunition she had found in Freddie's pocket. "We'd better get going," she said. "We're still no match for two men with automatic weapons."

"Give me a second to tie this bastard up," Quent said as he bent to do so. "We don't want him taking off before we can get hold of the constable. I'll tie his feet together, then bend him backward around the table leg and tie his hands and feet together. That ought to keep him here."

Freddie started to groan as Quent performed his ministrations with the rope. Quent had just finished when Freddie opened his eyes. "Hey, Quent," he said hoarsely, "cut it out, I'm one of the good guys."

"Like hell you are," Quent said, giving the rope an extra jerk to pull it tighter. "You're one of the lousiest bastards on the face of the earth."

"Ouch! I can see why you might feel that way," Freddie said, "but it's not what it looks like. I came back to let you two go, not kill you. I've even got Jepson coming with the Rolls to pick you up, bottle of champagne and all, in a few minutes."

"Don't make me laugh," Lyndsay said bitterly. "You must be crazy if you think we'd fall for that story. You're only trying to keep us here until those men with the automatic rifles come back."

"They aren't coming back. They've been set up. They're going to be arrested about a half hour from now, along with several other arms-smuggling groups around the country. It's a coordinated sting operation."

"Sure it is," Quent said dryly as he went to pick up the ladder and put it back in position. "And I'm jolly Santa Claus. Come on, Lyndsay, you go up first."

"If you're telling the truth," she said as she started up the ladder, "Constable Barnwell will tell us, and we'll come back for you. I'll even bring a bottle of champagne and personally break it over your head!"

"For God's sake, don't call Barnwell!" Freddie cried, his voice anguished. "He's one of them. That will tip him off and ruin everything!"

Lyndsay clambered out onto the floor above and looked back. Quent was standing by the ladder, looking back at Freddie. "Come on, Quent," she said. "Let's hurry."

"Just a minute," he said. "Maybe we ought to hear the rest of this."

"Oh, no!" Lyndsay cried, catching the sound of a vehicle creaking as it came down the bumpy road toward the old building. "Someone's coming!"

"Who is it?" Quent asked, coming rapidly up the ladder.

Lyndsay ran to the door and peeked out. "The Rolls," she croaked, weak with relief.

"Stay here while I check it out," Quent ordered. "For all we know, Jepson's a criminal, too."

The Rolls came to a stop in front of the building, but Jepson made no move to get out. Cautiously, Quent went over to the car and then jerked the door open, holding his gun on the startled chauffeur. Bug-eyed with fright, the man got out and let Quent inspect him and the vehicle. By the time that Quent returned, Lyndsay was laughing helplessly, the tears running down her cheeks.

"Everything's just as Freddie said it was," Quent said. "What's so funny?"

"The way Jepson looked," Lyndsay choked out, laughing even harder. "He was scared to death. I guess it's not really funny. Maybe I'm just hysterical. It's all been such a shock."

Quent put his arm around her and pulled her close against him. "Poor little angel," he said. "One thing's for certain. You're a lot braver than Jepson. Let's go down and see what Freddie has to say."

When they were back in the cellar, Quent said, "All right, let's hear the whole story."

"How about untying me first?" Freddie suggested. "It's harder than hell to talk in this position."

Quent shook his head. "Not until I'm satisfied you're telling the truth. After what you put Lyndsay through, maybe not even then."

Freddie groaned. "It'll blow my cover."

"I don't give a damn," Quent said impatiently. "Talk. Now!"

"All right, all right. I've been working undercover with British intelligence. Arms from Frobisher Munitions were being diverted, little bits of shipments, here and there. They showed up in Northern Ireland. I made some contacts, found out who and where, can't tell you how. Pretty soon, people trusted me to come up with bigger and better shipments. There are five small airfields, scattered around the country, where at precisely five-thirty this afternoon the smugglers will be set to load their contraband onto small aircraft, supposedly to zoom off fifteen minutes later. In reality, agents will be waiting to arrest those involved, including Constable Barnwell, who will be driving the lorry the weapons Lyndsay saw were transferred to." Freddie paused and frowned. "What time is it?"

"Almost five-thirty," Quent replied. "We should be able to check out your story very shortly."

"Then how about letting me up?" Freddie asked plaintively.

"Not just yet," Lyndsay said coldly. "You still haven't explained why you did what you did to us. Why didn't you just tell us what was going on?"

Freddie groaned again. "With those men here? I'm supposed to take a chance they'll suspect that something's rotten in Denmark? Besides, after what you'd seen, would you have believed me?"

"Maybe I wouldn't have," Lyndsay replied, "but Quent might if you'd let me loose before he got here, instead of holding a gun to my head."

"I couldn't take the chance," Freddie replied. "I had to get him here and out of the way as fast as I could so that I could send the signal to the agents that we'd gotten loaded here on schedule. I was sure he'd be along and mess everything up if I didn't."

"Would you have?" Lyndsay asked, glancing at Quent. "I wasn't sure you'd come looking for me at all after this morning."

Quent smiled. "I had a talk with Marian, and she straightened me out on several things. Freddie caught me just as I was going out the door. It saved me looking for you, anyway." He put his arms around Lyndsay and held her tightly, burying his face in her hair. "What do you say, love?" he asked. "Shall we let the rascal go?"

Lyndsay sighed, nestling contentedly against Quent's broad chest. "I suppose so, but I wish you didn't have to let go of me to let him go."

"So do I," Quent said. "Maybe we should make him wait a while longer. We could send someone back to get him."

"I say now, that's not fair!" Freddie exclaimed from the floor. "After all, I brought you two together. Everything lovey-dovey again, and all that. Not to mention my good offices as the Gravelpick ghost."

Lyndsay laughed and looked at Quent. "He does have a point," she said.

Quent quickly untied Freddie's knots and helped him up. "There you go. Are you all right to drive?"

"Fit as a fiddle," Freddie replied. "How about giving me my gun back? It isn't loaded."

"It isn't?" Quent flipped the chamber open. "It isn't." He handed the gun to Freddie. "What, pray tell, were you carrying an unloaded gun for?"

Freddie grinned. "Safer that way. Oh, it was loaded when Lyndsay got here, but I unloaded it before I came back. I was toying with the idea of holding it to your head until you said some things to Lyndsay that she wants to hear, but I gather you've at least made a start in the right direction."

Lyndsay looked up at Quent and smiled. "Shall we tell him?"

"Let me guess," Freddie said, looking from one smiling face to the other. "You're going to be married. That's marvelous. Good heavens, I feel like Cupid. First thing you know, I'll be running around naked with a bow and arrow. Well, don't just stand there laughing. Let's get back and tell Aunt Marian. But watch out. She'll start planning the wedding before you even get the words out."

LYNDSAY AND QUENT were laughing again an hour later when Marian shooed them off upstairs with strict orders not to show their faces until the next morning.

"I like Auntie's subtlety, don't you?" Freddie said. "You *will* have a romantic evening, come hell or high water."

"It's not that at all," Marian retorted. "They deserve to be alone. I'm sure they've had enough of other people's company, especially yours. Tomorrow's soon enough to start planning the wedding."

"See? What did I tell you?" Freddie said.

Even Sofia was beaming when, after Lyndsay and Quent had had time to bathe, she brought their dinner to Quent's room, complete with an iced bottle of champagne and a huge bouquet of Marian's precious roses.

"Congratulations on your engagement. Have a lovely evening," she said as she left the room.

"I guess even Sofia's a romantic at heart," Lyndsay mused aloud.

"I pity those who aren't," Quent said. He smiled wryly. "Of course, some people go a bit overboard, namely Luke and my sister. I didn't need quite that much help."

"Oh, I don't know," Lyndsay said, giving him a mischievous smile. "Here we are engaged in just two days, thanks to them. Admit it. It might have taken you months without it."

Quent grinned. "Okay, I admit it. This is better." He picked up the bottle of champagne and first looked at it, then over at the big bed, where someone had thoughtfully piled half a dozen extra pillows. "Shall we drink a little toast to our future and then go and snuggle up together for a while? I'm a lot hungrier to hold you than I am for food right now."

"That's a perfect idea," Lyndsay agreed.

Quent popped the cork and poured them each a flute of bubbling liquid. "To us," he said, touching his glass to Lyndsay's.

"To us," she echoed, smiling into the glowing warmth of Quent's beautiful jade-green eyes.

"You know something, sweetheart?" he said, kissing her lips softly and tucking her close against him as they luxuriated in the soft mound of pillows. "You may think I'm crazy to say this, but I think I'm almost glad we had that miserable experience this afternoon. I learned some things I needed to know."

"What things are those, my love?" Lyndsay asked, gingerly touching the scrape on Quent's cheek he had gotten when Freddie felled him. "Does that hurt?"

"Not a bit." Quent caught Lyndsay's hand and held it against his cheek. "I learned I can't protect you all the time, and I also learned how strong and courageous you are. I'll never forget the look in your eyes when I first saw you there, tied to that chair, with a gun at your head. It was all love and courage and—" his voice broke and his eyes became misty "—all I could think was what a fool I'd been not to tell you how much I loved you before. I was looking for a guarantee of the future and letting day after day slip by. You can try to plan ahead, but all you really have is now. And I want now and forever with you."

"Oh, Quent," Lyndsay said, her voice choked with tears of happiness, "I love you so much." She flung her arms around his neck, and suddenly their mouths were together, and they devoured each other with an explosion of passion and relief. Shimmering waves of joy and excitement flooded Lyndsay's body as Quent's hands gently caressed her, sending her soaring into a world of boundless sunshine and tingling, crystal clear air. "I'm flying," she whispered as Quent's lips left hers and moved down her neck with downy soft kisses.

"So am I," he answered, his voice deep with longing. He raised his head and stared into her eyes as his hands untied the belt of her robe. He pushed her robe apart and then unfastened his own, watching her intently, his dark-centered eyes filled with fiery sparks, yet gentle and loving. "Remember when I wanted to pretend we were doing this?" he whispered.

Lyndsay smiled. "I remember."

"Shall we stop pretending?" Quent asked.

"Yes," Lyndsay said softly.

Quent's smile of happiness set Lyndsay's heart racing. What a wonderful, loving, gentle man he was. She held on to his broad shoulders as he slowly lowered himself upon her, revelling in the thrill of each new touch of bare skin against bare skin. For a moment he lay still, his cheek against hers. Lyndsay could feel his heart pounding, strong and regular, could feel the hard evidence of his desire. Time seemed suspended, the world made of sensations of electricity and heat that grew ever stronger. Then Quent lifted his head and covered her mouth with his once again. His hands explored her body, firing new sparks wherever they touched. Erratic patterns merged into a rhythm, the rhythm into a symphony of movement. Each time Lyndsay felt that surely she had reached the crescendo, that she could fly no higher, she found she was wrong, until at last one final, pulsing beat sent her spiraling over the top and let her spin in ever-widening circles back to earth.

"I think I'm in heaven," Lyndsay murmured against Quent's neck as he rolled to the side, still holding her close.

"I know I am," Quent said. "I'm holding an angel."

Lyndsay leaned her head back against his shoulder and smiled at him. "You say the sweetest things," she said. "I remember once you said you thought I might be Cinderella, who'd disappear at midnight, and another time you said you thought we were in Camelot." She looked around at the huge, centuries-old room. "I think I still feel like I'm in Camelot."

"It does seem a bit unreal, doesn't it?" Quent said. "Maybe that's because it's part of one of Luke's fancies." He sighed and looked at Lyndsay thoughtfully. "I guess I'm grateful to that rascal, after all. He's a regular magician."

"He's our Merlin," Lyndsay said. She looked up at Quent, suddenly feeling anxious. "He can't make this all disappear, can he? I'm not just dreaming?"

"Oh, darling love, of course not," Quent said, his arms crushing her to him. "I'll be here when you go to sleep and still be here when you wake up from now on, as long as I live." He smiled at Lyndsay, his eyes so bright with love she caught her breath. "I may not live forever," he said, "but as long as I have you with me, I'll give it one heck of a try."

Tears of happiness filled Lyndsay's eyes. "I'll be here," she promised. "Always."

EPILOGUE

THE SOUND of the clock booming out twelve noon was clearly audible in the palatial grand salon at Gravelpick Manor, which had been transformed into a flower-filled wedding chapel by Marian and an army of workers. All of Lyndsay and Quent's families were there, as well as Angie, transported across the Atlantic at Sir Alfred's expense so that his beloved Marian could have the pleasure of putting on the wedding.

"Damn, I wish I hadn't brought that blasted clock back," Freddie muttered under his breath to Quent, as he stood beside him at the altar. "It sounds like the tolling of doomsday."

Quent looked down at Freddie and grinned. "What are you so nervous about? I'm the one who's getting married."

"My days are numbered," Freddie replied. "I can feel it in my bones." He fidgeted nervously. "Why don't they get started?"

"They are," Quent said, turning to watch as the strains of the "Wedding March" from *Lohengrin* rang out. "Isn't she beautiful?" he whispered as he caught his first glimpse of Lyndsay in her elegant gown of chiffon and lace.

"That she is," Freddie, whose eyes were on Angie Bielema, agreed.

Luke and Theresa Thorndike turned to watch Lyndsay, smiling radiantly as she walked slowly along on her father's arm.

"Marvelous, isn't it?" Luke whispered in Theresa's ear. "They didn't suspect a thing."

Lyndsay's eyes met Theresa's and she gave her an extra warm smile. What a terrific friend, she thought. And now they were going to be sisters. As she passed Theresa, she tucked a folded note into her hand and then turned all her attention to the handsome man waiting for her at the altar.

Theresa unfolded the note, read it, then looked at Luke with her eyebrows raised. "So they didn't suspect anything, hmm?" she whispered, handing him the note.

"Theresa and Luke—nice work. Thanks a million. Lyndsay and Quent," Luke read under his breath. "Maybe they're just thanking us for getting them the job?" he suggested.

"Not likely, after what they went through," Theresa said, shaking her head. "I hope you've learned your lesson."

Luke grinned unrepentantly. "Of course, dear," he said.

Theresa sighed. Luke hadn't learned at all, she knew. He was hopelessly romantic. But, she thought, tears filling her eyes as her brother, his face glowing with happiness, took his bride into his arms, why shouldn't he be? So far, he had helped four people find happiness. Who knew how many more there might be?

Luke leaned over to whisper in Theresa's ear again. "Have you noticed how Freddie keeps staring at that blonde from Quent's office?"

Let
HARLEQUIN ROMANCE®
take you

BACK TO THE

Come to the Ferris Ranch in the
San Luis Valley, Colorado.

Meet Greg Ferris, a handsome, easygoing rancher and
his wife (almost *ex-wife!*), Stacy Hamelton.

Read THE COWBOY NEXT DOOR by Jeanne Allan,
author of the popular RANCHER'S BRIDE.
Available in October 1993
wherever Harlequin Books are sold.

RANCH-5

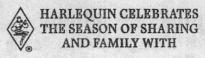

HARLEQUIN CELEBRATES
THE SEASON OF SHARING
AND FAMILY WITH

Harlequin introduces the latest member in its family of
seasonal collections. Following in the footsteps of the popular
My Valentine, Just Married and *Harlequin Historical Christmas
Stories*, we are proud to present FRIENDS, FAMILIES,
LOVERS. A collection of three new contemporary romance
stories about America at its best, about welcoming others into
the circle of love.... Stories to warm your heart ...

By three leading romance authors:

> KATHLEEN EAGLE
> SANDRA KITT
> RUTH JEAN DALE

> Available in October, wherever
> Harlequin books are sold.

THANKS

HARLEQUIN ROMANCE®

A Halloween treat that's better than candy and
almost as good as a kiss!

Two delightful frightful Romances from two of our
most popular authors:

HAUNTED SPOUSE by Heather Allison
(Harlequin Romance 3284)
"Frizzy Lizzie" the Scream Queen confronts her
handsome ex-husband—over a haunted house!

TO CATCH A GHOST by Day Leclaire
(Harlequin Romance 3285)
Zach Kingston wants to debunk Rachel Avery's
family ghost. Rachel objects—and so does the
ghost!

Available in October—just in time for
Halloween!—wherever Harlequin books are sold.

Calloway Corners

In September, Harlequin is proud to bring readers four involving, romantic stories about the Calloway sisters, set in Calloway Corners, Louisiana. Written by four of Harlequin's most popular and award-winning authors, you'll be enchanted by these sisters and the men they love!

MARIAH by Sandra Canfield
JO by Tracy Hughes
TESS by Katherine Burton
EDEN by Penny Richards

As an added bonus, you can enter a sweepstakes contest to win a trip to Calloway Corners, and meet all four authors. Watch for details in all Calloway Corners books in September.

CAL93

Fifty red-blooded, white-hot, true-blue hunks from every State in the Union!

Beginning in May, look for MEN MADE IN AMERICA! Written by some of our most popular authors, these stories feature fifty of the strongest, sexiest men, each from a different state in the union!

Two titles available every other month at your favorite retail outlet.

In September, look for:

DECEPTIONS by Annette Broadrick (California)
STORMWALKER by Dallas Schulze (Colorado)

In November, look for:

STRAIGHT FROM THE HEART by Barbara Delinsky (Connecticut)
AUTHOR'S CHOICE by Elizabeth August (Delaware)

You won't be able to resist MEN MADE IN AMERICA!